THE
MONSTER
OF HER AGE

ALSO BY DANIELLE BINKS

Begin, End, Begin: A #LoveOzYA Anthology
The Year the Maps Changed

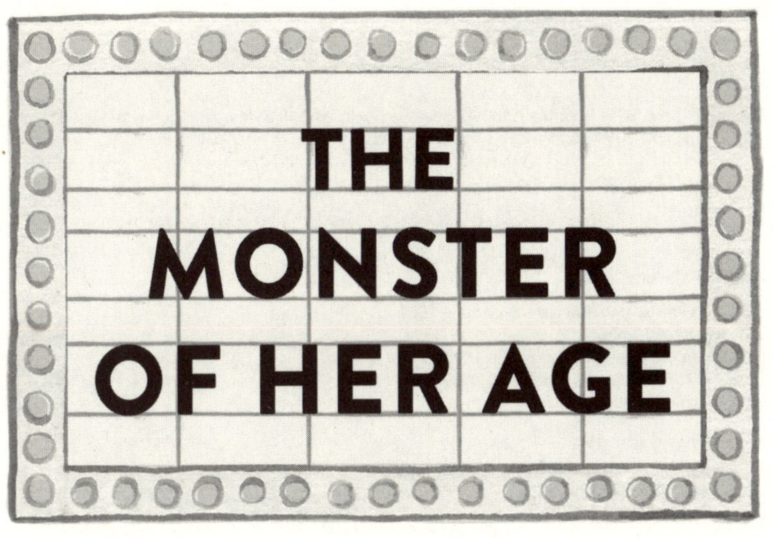

Danielle Binks

LOTHIAN

This is a work of fiction. All central characters are fictional, and any resemblance to actual persons is entirely coincidental. In order to provide the story with a context, real names of places are used as well as some significant historical events. A number of high-profile people are also referred to, but there is no suggestion that the events described concerning the fictional characters ever occurred.

The quote on p. 82 is from the Anna Akhmatova poem 'You Will Hear Thunder' and is used with permission. Anna Akhmatova's rights are acquired via FTM Agency Ltd, Russia.

A Lothian Children's Book

Published in Australia and New Zealand in 2021
by Hachette Australia
(an imprint of Hachette Australia Pty Limited)
Level 17, 207 Kent Street, Sydney NSW 2000
www.hachettechildrens.com.au

10 9 8 7 6 5 4 3 2 1

A catalogue record for this book is available from the National Library of Australia

ISBN: 978 0 7344 1973 6 (paperback)

Cover design by Christabella Designs
Cover illustrations by Anne Barnetson
Author photo by Janis House, Janis House Photography
Typeset in 11.2/16.1 pt Minion Pro by Bookhouse, Sydney
Printed and bound in Australia by McPherson's Printing Group

The paper this book is printed on is certified against the Forest Stewardship Council® Standards. McPherson's Printing Group holds FSC® chain of custody certification SA-COC-005379. FSC® promotes environmentally responsible, socially beneficial and economically viable management of the world's forests.

Nanna, Omi & Aunty Pat –
and all the matriarchs that make us.

For Don & Helga too
– Pop & Big H –
the strongest pillars in our family, always.

A NOTE ON REPRESENTATION WITHIN

In scenes featuring the character Jen, you'll notice I've used an upper-case 'D' for Deaf. This was a deliberate choice to highlight that Jen identifies as culturally Deaf, which means she shares a common culture and sign language with the Deaf community. For Jen, as for many people, Deafness is not just a medical diagnosis or a deficit that needs to be 'fixed', but a way of engaging with the world.

ACKNOWLEDGEMENT OF COUNTRY

This fictional story is set on the land of nipaluna (Hobart). I acknowledge with deep respect that sovereignty was never ceded, and the traditional and rightful owners of this land are the muwinina people. I pay respect to those who have passed before us and acknowledge today's Tasmanian Aboriginal people, who are the custodians of this land – always.

I shall thus give a general answer to the question, so frequently asked me: 'How I, then a young girl, came to think of, and to dilate upon, so very hideous an idea?'

—Mary Shelley's Introduction to the 1831 edition of *Frankenstein*

The Exorcist has been a very interesting cross to bear.

—Linda Blair

ONE

Growing up, Lottie looked just the same to me as she did in the movies.

I'd recognise her instantly when she marched onto our television screen in the Midday Movie Classic. To everyone else she was a leading lady and film legend but to me she was Lottie – my grandmother, my *bubbe*. Mum had trained me to blow her a kiss, or wave my chubby hands at her on the TV. And when I was very young, I'd get frustrated that Lottie would never wave back or speak to me. I could never break that stride.

My favourite moment was from her 1987 film, *Seven Hills,* where she played a glamorous ghost. I loved this particular scene at the Ripponlea mansion pool at night, with softly lit lamps flickering in the arches. A party can be heard tinkling inside, and a man in a white suit walks around the sandstone edge, sipping from a glass. Then Lottie suddenly appears, emerging from the shadows, startling him so he sloshes his entire highball into the water. There's this beautiful shot of the tumbler sinking, and then gently clinking upright to the tiled sea-green bottom – all while the waterlogged sound of the party continues up above.

The scene cuts again, and the viewer is coaxed back by the sound of Lottie's laugh, and then the whole production of her taking a seat by the fountain – sweeping out the slinky black gown she was buried in and arranging herself on the edge. The camera zooms in, just as she arches one of her brows at him. She asks, 'Did I scare you, darling?' Then there's a cut away as she starts swirling her fingers in the water. 'Good,' she says, as the camera pans out to show that she's not making ripples. 'A man like you could use a little fright in his life.'

And it's the way she purrs that 'good', how it rumbles out of her in that incomparable Lovinger lilt – you can practically feel the vibrations along your spine.

It gets me every time.

And I wonder if this is how I can choose to remember my grandmother.

Just as she was in the movies.

TWO

Sadness has stages. In Judaism, mourning (*Aveilut*) does too: *Aninut, Sheloshim, Shanah, Yahrzeit, Yizkor.* These are the helpful guidelines and parameters to our grief: for organising burial, the funeral itself, returning home from the cemetery, the first year of bereavement, unveiling the gravestone and then the anniversary of the death.

But there's nothing, really, no steps or processes, obligations or rituals, for the time before that. When a person is neither living nor dead but just . . . existing. Barely holding on.

And this is where my *bubbe* is right now. She is caught between the worlds of living and dying, even as she's also on the TV screen, in the corner of her hospital room.

It feels a little bit like witchcraft, or else reminds me of being a toddler again, blinking at the screen and the image of my glamourised and younger grandmother, and then turning my head to look at her walking around our house barefoot, a silk hairscarf hiding her silver-streaked auburn locks.

Both there and not. Real and imaginary.

Did I scare you, darling?

'Good,' Corinne, Lottie's nurse, says, trying to imitate her low rumble. And then a beat too quickly she says, 'A man like you could use a little fright in his life.'

A man like you could use a little fright in his life, a much-younger Lottie echoes eerily from the screen, which hangs from a bracket in the corner of the room.

'I love that part,' Corinne says, and then she turns to Lottie, whose eyes are closed but whose chest rises and falls steadily. 'I love that part, Lottie – and I love this movie.'

Then Corinne looks straight at me, and I force a smile.

'Thanks, she'd really like to hear that,' I say, even though I have no idea if that's true.

'Well, I told her so when she first came in, I said, "*Seven Hills* was up there for me, but *The Hazards* was the first R-rated movie I ever saw and I just love it more!" I told her my older brother's best friend snuck us into the theatre.'

Corinne shakes her head and smiles, seemingly at the memory as she continues to slowly massage my grandmother's wrists one at a time. She gently pulls on each finger, applying moisturiser but also stretching and limbering her, as though she's Play-Doh that's been left out too long and needs to be worked back into something more malleable.

'I love that part in *The Hazards* where she and her husband have to get onto the roof of the school, and they look out at all the little lights of the town . . .'

I'm nodding my head and smiling, the same smile from when she first started talking to me and I can feel it starting to twitch at the edges.

'. . . and she slings that cricket bat onto her shoulder and just looks, y'know? And she's covered in all that blood and crap, and they've still got to go and kill more of those living-dead, but they're just taking a moment to breathe it all in, and I remember turning to my friend Tony in that moment and saying, "I'm going to be a palliative care nurse one day."'

I blink and my smile falls.

Corinne glances up at me just as she's pulling on the pinky of Lottie's left hand, and she chuckles. 'I'm kidding,' she says. 'I told your grandma that same joke and I thought I was going to have to get the oxygen tank for her, she laughed so much.'

Corinne lets go of Lottie's hands, folding them gently one on top of the other on her chest, where the blanket covers her.

I fidget uncomfortably in the wing chair they've placed by the window, within arm's reach of her bed. I clear my throat and ask, 'So she was able to talk, when she first came in?'

Corinne reaches for a tissue and wipes off the excess moisturiser from her hands. She's a short woman, and I'm trying to calculate her age if she saw *The Hazards* illicitly when it first came out in cinemas and guesstimate that she must be in her mid-40s, but she looks a lot younger.

'She had some paralysis and slurring of words but she was able to communicate a little,' Corrine says, and gives me a small, but sad smile.

That was two days ago.

Three days before, she'd been in the kitchen when she suddenly fell to the floor. It was pure luck that she and my uncle Jasper had scheduled lunch together and he'd been in the house to hear the shattering of a glass she'd been holding as she fell.

She'd had a hemorrhagic stroke, a bleed on the brain.

Mum had already been in transit from London to Melbourne, coming to pick me up from my boarding school in Mt Eliza and drag me to Hobart, because I'd run out of excuses to stay away.

The Head of House came to get me from the rec room in the middle of the afternoon on a Saturday while I was playing billiards with Aiya. My first thought was to be mortified that maybe Mum was having me kicked out of school before end of term, just to make sure I'd have nowhere else to go but home. But then Margaret – Mags, we called her, my Head of House – said Mum was on the phone and wanted to talk to me.

The whole way to Mags' office I kept wondering why Mum wouldn't just call me on my mobile instead of the literal old-school landline I'd never even heard ring before. And then I wondered why Mags was closing the office door behind her and taking a seat on the two-seater couch in her office, preparing to listen to our conversation.

I swallowed down the instinct I had to accuse Mum of not taking my side and forcing me to go home with her again. Of not listening when I said I wasn't ready.

Instead, I sat down at Mags' desk chair, brought the phone up to my ear. The weight of it had me balancing an elbow on the table and cradling it to hear the tinny sound of our school choir singing a song from *Sweet Charity* recorded during school assembly a few weeks ago.

Mags must have heard it then too, because she rose up off the couch and reached over to hit a button – cutting off a 'Go forth' – and letting me hear Mum sigh into the phone and breathe my name. 'Ellie, are you there?'

She'd found out during layover in Bangkok. Dad had been trying to get hold of her, and then Uncle Jasper had rung and told her that Lottie would be going into emergency surgery the next day. She hadn't wanted to tell me straight away and in the middle of the night but now she was in Melbourne and calling me to say she was getting on the next flight to Hobart leaving in twenty minutes, and I'd have to make my own way home.

There was no room for protesting, or even questioning. Mum had never sounded so far away and I remember sitting in that little office with the heavy phone pressed to my ear. I remember the pull my body felt to already be there. To be here, with Mum and Lottie.

'Ellie?' she'd said. 'Darling, I just need you to know . . . she's probably not going to wake up again.'

I let out a breath I didn't know I'd been holding, and absurdly started to say, 'I lost . . .' but then an announcement came over a loud-speaker at the airport, and Mum couldn't hear me, asked me to repeat what I'd said – but instead I blinked, and told her I was on my way.

I don't even know what I'd been trying to say. Only that I had this feeling of time getting away from me, like it was a piece of me that had in that moment broken away, just dislodged or chipped off. And yes, I felt like I'd lost something of myself – that being out of time was much like being emptied of the possibilities it brings.

Or something.

Mum, meanwhile, arrived just in time. She got there and sat with Lottie for a bit before the surgery to relieve the pressure on her brain. But that's all it was – relief, not cure. They could stop the worst of the bleeding that would have been causing her headaches and could have led to more seizures, but there was no chance of recovery and slimmer still of her ever waking up again.

They put her on morphine and hooked her up to a bunch of machines and called it end-of-life care, but there was no deadline on when the end would come. It could be any second, or weeks from now.

And it's not quite true, about there being no rules for dying. We don't do last rites, but there is the final confessional prayer (*Viduy*) and we are supposed to find out what the person wants, and if they have any final concerns that can be eased. They're also not supposed to die alone – which seems like an impossible task, to me – and finally, nothing can be done that might hasten the dying process.

And these not-quite-rules for not-quite-living are the whole reason I'm here.

'Knock, knock.'

Corinne and I both look to the door, where my uncle Jasper is standing. He's tall and lanky with dishevelled, thinning hair, and a kind, if ordinary, face. He'd be typecast as an accountant if he'd had any inclination to follow in his famous mother's footsteps, but luckily, he leaned into the role most fully and became a tax lawyer instead. Right now he's got an armful of newspapers and magazines, and he's brought a thermos of what smells like his favourite Swiss brew coffee.

'Changeover time,' he says, and grimaces – it's his attempt at a smile, a gesture to fill in the pleasantries of how strange all this is; that I'm tapping out of sitting by my grandmother's deathbed, while he's tapping in to sit with his mother as she's slowly dying.

I stand up and roll my head, feeling for a crack, which makes Jasper wince when he hears my neck vertebrae give a satisfying pop. Corinne checks a bunch of Lottie's machines, and Jasper lumbers around to my side of the room to take my place in the wing chair, which he folds himself into.

And the whole time Lottie Lovinger has been traipsing around the Ripponlea estate on the TV in the corner, making a living man fall in love with her glamourous, ghostly self.

Maybe other people in Lottie's position would want music on, or a noise machine but we all figured that keeping the TV on Turner Classic Movies (TMC) would let her hear some old friends, relatives and relive some memories too, like *Seven Hills*.

Maybe it's just the reminder she needs right now that no matter what happens over the coming days and weeks as her body winds down, the show will always be going on somewhere in the world for the infamous Lottie Lovinger.

THREE

It's a short walk from Creswell Private Hospital to Battery Point. Jasper offered me his car to take home, but I wanted to walk and get reacquainted.

I was born and grew up in Hobart. When I was 13, my parents and I moved to London for two years. Then I came back to Australia to board at a school on the outskirts of Melbourne, where I've been for three years with the occasional trips back to England and my parents for Christmas and family holidays. I haven't returned to Hobart since I started boarding, but it's not for lack of trying and bribing on my family's part.

The latest of these negotiations happened in the last week of June this year, the first week of winter school holidays. My mother had let it be known that Lottie was hoping I'd agree to stay with her in Hobart for a portion of my break and, with a mind to beyond, when my studies concluded, perhaps I'd think about moving home to Hobart again permanently. I'd flatly refused, and then proceeded to hang around the boarding school house in Mt Eliza with my fellow boarders who were also disinclined to return to their respective corners of the world.

An armistice was reached via my father, who said Lottie would be in Melbourne for one day only to attend a show at the Arts Centre. And so the Hopetoun Tea Rooms were chosen as the location for a détente, on strict understanding that I wouldn't be returning to Hobart anytime soon and no one could make me, least of all Lottie – my very reason for staying away.

I deliberately arrived twenty minutes late to the Tea Rooms in the Block Arcade, with its emerald-green leaf wallpaper, shaded chandeliers, blackwood panelling and rows and rows of cakes lit up for display in the large front window. My grandmother was sitting among all this 128-year-old cramped opulence, at a table in a back corner of the room. She was facing away from the many fellow diners, with the greater chance of privacy the far wall afforded.

Her thick, dark-auburn hair was instantly recognisable, even in a neat chignon that emphasised that she now had more stripes of silver. She was dressed in a side-wrap crisp white shirt, with a black peacoat hanging from the back of her chair. I wound my way carefully through the labyrinth of little tables until I got to hers. Then I stopped, took a deep breath and moved to pull out the chair opposite her. I didn't bother to remove my own coat, even if its oversized pufferness was hot and awkward sitting in the dainty chair, and she raised an eyebrow at my continuing to wear it.

'Ellie,' she said, 'thank you for agreeing to meet with me.'

I didn't acknowledge this greeting, nor did I need to. Lottie had already turned and caught the eye of a waitress. She raised her manicured hand in the air and nodded, which triggered the bringing over of a chocolate-raspberry Swiss roll on a delicate china plate that was placed in front of me.

'Your favourite, if I remember correctly,' she said, and poured herself a cup of Earl Grey tea from a pot that had been sitting on the table.

I'd known why she opted for Hopetoun. This place was part of a ritual when I was very young and my grandmother was in a production at the Princess Theatre, or else filming around the city. If she was away for long enough, she'd insist on my parents and me – or else just me and Mum – coming up for a weekend to spend time with her, and a visit to the Tea Rooms was always a little expedition for just her and me, followed by a trip to Dymocks on Collins Street for book-buying treats.

'Do you remember the first time . . .' Lottie began.

'Can we not?' I interrupted, then I picked up one of the little forks and stabbed it into the Swiss roll, breaking off a chunk of chocolate and shovelling it into my mouth.

Lottie placed her teacup very gently on its saucer, then crossed her arms in front of her and lay them flat on the table, still keeping her back perfectly postured and straight as she levelled me with her dark-green gaze.

My grandmother had, of course, always looked old to me. Not in the way she dressed because at some point she'd decided to channel a sort of Katharine Hepburn vibe of tailored pants and comfortable shirts, favouring Australian designers for a timeless Hartford-to-Hobart aesthetic. But for a while, she seemed to have been frozen in time as the typecast refined grandmother and matriarch – still with high cheekbones, perfectly sculpted brows, and dignified laugh-lines about her eyes and at the corners of her mouth, painted in classic Charlotte Tilbury 'Stoned Rose' lipstick shade.

But suddenly sitting before her and not having come face-to-face for quite some time, she looked all of her 76 years, to me. The minimal amount of refined make-up could not hide the slightly sunken cheeks, papery complexion or a new tiredness behind her eyes. And then she let out a sigh and I wondered if it was me who was ageing her suddenly – that her tiredness was more about my proximity, the thought of which made me angry.

'I've let things get away from us.' She shook her head. 'I've let you go on too long in your fit of pique, and now I think it's time we moved forward, you and I. We cannot go back in time, nor can I erase what happened. I can only tell you that I will never be able to forgive myself . . .'

I scoffed and cut her off. 'Well, that's a relief, because I wasn't intending to forgive you either.'

Lottie blinked at me, and I took the opportunity to slice off another piece of chocolate roll. It was then that I felt a prickling of attention on my right side. I looked up and could tell from the way she was looking at me that Lottie felt it too. There were eyeballs on us, and we could both sense the hum of awareness that comes from somebody recognising you, whispering your name, which could be heard even above the low-level roar that filled the small room, packed to the brim with other patrons chattering. I imagine it must be how hunted animals feel in the wild, but instead of the cock of a gun, it's the shuttered sound of a camera-phone going off.

I watched as a veil fell over my grandmother's face, and one I knew well; her lips lifted in a radiant smile that somehow brought the roundness back to her cheeks and a twinkle to her eye, like the light was really reaching them. When she turned and cocked her head slightly at a couple, probably in their mid-50s and clearly foreign tourists, two tables away from us, the gentleman was quick to lower the phone that was aimed our way.

Lottie mouthed the words 'excuse me' to the two tables of couples, who barely glanced at us, between us and them. And then she looked at the man and the woman and said with a brittle politeness, 'Do you mind, we'd really prefer . . .'

But the woman was already jumping up and coming our way, bumping a chair as she passed and earning a scowl from a fellow diner.

'We really are the *biggest* fans!' she said in a thick midwestern American accent, her hands outstretched in pleading.

I tried to shrink more into my puffer jacket, but it felt like the mere movement of trying to dissolve into the lush, green wallpaper caused the woman to notice me and stop an arm's-length from our table as she looked between me and Lottie.

'Oh, I can't believe it. Oh *gosh*, David!' She turned back around to her partner, who wasn't vacating his seat because he was hemmed in on one side by shopping bags, and on the other by a new table of diners just arrived. So she forgot him and quickly turned back to us. 'I've just got to tell you that your movies have meant so much to me over the years,' she began, and it was then that people at other tables started turning their heads and raising their eyebrows. Not so much recognising Lottie or me, but rather intrigued by a general scent of celebrity in the air.

Feeling the ripple of awareness, Lottie quickly offered to take a selfie. I shook my head at the strangeness of hearing my grandmother utter that word, before clearing my throat and offering to take the photo instead.

I thought the woman's face was going to split in two, she was smiling so wide as she bent down beside Lottie, who gave her usual demure and tight smile. When I handed the woman her phone back, she stood up straight and looked at me intently. 'You'd lasso the moon just so you could hang it round my neck like a noose, Nanna,' she spoke in a truly terrible twang of an Australian accent, meant to be an imitation of me. And then looking between me and Lottie and snapping back to herself, she said, 'I loved your movie, with the both of you! I do hope you do something together again because it was just so nice to see.' Then she laughed, self-consciously. 'Not that it was a *nice* movie, I nearly peed my pants watching it on the couch!' Her hand flew to her mouth and she blushed deep red.

'Well, thank you kindly,' Lottie said, dismissively and the woman scuttled away. And then the two of us were left, now with the elephant in the room caught between us.

Or maybe, the werewolf in the room would be more appropriate.

I am of course talking about the movie in question – *Blood & Jacaranda*.

You've no doubt heard of it. I was, after all, last year voted No. 8 in *Reel Magazine*'s Top 50 Scariest Monsters in Movie History. I was beaten by Skarsgård's Pennywise from *It*, but deemed scarier than *The Babadook*. Not bad for being eleven years old at the time of filming my one and only role playing 'Little Mate' – an abused werewolf child on a rural Adelaide commune. *Blood & Jacaranda* was an Oz indie horror movie, a slow-burn with audiences on release. Then it hit streaming services and became a wildfire. It's something to scorch me still – and right then, in that moment, I felt the familiar hot creep up my neck, stealing breath from my lungs so I had to breathe sharply in through my nose and let it out in a sigh. Then I clambered to push the chair back and rose from the table.

Lottie called to me, but her voice seemed far away and then got more distant as I started weaving my way through the room again and heading towards the door.

I came out on Collins Street and began walking vaguely in the direction of Flinders Street Station. I had every intention of boarding the next train to Frankston and reenforcing my blackout cold-shouldering of Lottie, when I felt a hand reach out and grab my elbow and stop me.

I think she was surprised that I did stop, and so she rushed to shrug on her peacoat and then hustled us both off the footpath. We were beside a London plane tree and I briefly considered blaming my stinging eyes and running nose on allergies, but I thought my grandmother would see through such a poor performance. And then she reached into one of her deep pockets and produced a handkerchief – monogrammed 'LL' and everything – and handed it to me.

'Even after all this time, Ellie?' Lottie said, and then she sighed. 'What do you intend to do with yourself, now that school is ending for you? Get underfoot in London while your parents are working? Take one of those useless "gap years" your generation invented?' she huffed. 'Come with me to Hobart. Let's finally have this out and get you home, and then we can . . .'

I thrust the handkerchief back at her, having wiped my eyes with it, and used my own coat sleeve for my nose, mostly to see her wince when I did.

'You know what's just *perfect*? I mean, really bang-on for accuracy?' I asked, not waiting for a reply. 'Calling a film "cult classic" to describe truly twisted devotion to something so terrible . . .'

Lottie opened her mouth to say something, but I pressed on.

'And how accurate that our film has that pedigree, right? The great Lottie Lovinger and granddaughter together in a movie that ironically, destroyed our family.'

'Ellie! Don't say that . . .'

'Why not? It's true.' I shrugged. 'Worth the cult status, do you think?'

Lottie reached out a hand to me, but I thrust mine into my pockets and moved away, then I turned and started walking. She may have called out to me again, I don't remember – but she didn't follow.

That was the first time I'd seen my grandmother in years – and, as it turns out, the last time I ever spoke to her.

And in the end, she did find a way to get me home to Hobart.

•

It turns out that I've missed my city – a deep-down missing I didn't even fully realise and can't quite explain, until I'd started walking its streets again. Each step feels like it is grounding and giving me a firmer hold on being home. And it's why I want to take the long way from the hospital back to Lovinger House now.

I take the scenic route past the Maritime Museum, Constitution Dock, Franklin Square, Parliament House and St David's Park. I walk up and down the old winding streets of Battery Point with their little cottages of Old Hobart Town, sitting alongside new and old colonial and revival homes with three-million-dollar views.

Warm September winds blow me along until I find myself walking painfully familiar trails, like a bruise I can't stop poking. I walk past my one-disastrous-year-only high school on Queen Street that's two minutes from home. The sandstone structure of the private co-ed school makes my heart beat fast with memories I'm surprised still have a hold over me – but I shouldn't be. I know better than most that some hurts can haunt you. It doesn't matter at what age they happened because they find a way to grow with you and around you, like a weed.

And I marvel at how loving and missing a place that still holds painful memories is that much harder when your family tree has deep roots in a city like Hobart and your family history and history itself are so deeply entwined . . . I think on this as I walk the hill to home and Lovinger House, which has been in my family for generations.

It was built in 1880 and was once even a zoo for thylacines – otherwise known as 'Tasmanian tigers' – before they became extinct. One of my lesser-known but no less great-great-uncles was a vaudeville actor whose wife was a passionate conservationist and turned a portion of the estate into a menagerie. That was torn down a long time ago, but she had a cast-iron statue made of one of those beautiful striped tiger-dog creatures and it is still paused in prowl, beneath a yellow wattle tree.

Overall, it's more manor than house, and more rundown than it deserves but it's been home to Lovingers since 1890. It has eleven bedrooms, nine bathrooms, and is situated on a little hill at the corner of Cromwell and Napoleon streets in Battery Point (what my uncle Jasper jokes is an 'uprising'), with clear views of both timtumili minanya, the River Derwent – and kunanyi/Mount Wellington.

Tourist buses lumber their way through the narrow, heritage streets of Battery Point every three hours, starting from 9 a.m. If you happen to be standing at our wrought-iron gates when one goes by at quarter-past, you'll hear the tour guide say our house is an example of the 'Victorian Gothic Revival style of the time,' before launching into a brief history of the Famous Lovinger Theatrical Family, some of whom still reside here – *to this day.*

And I don't need to pull my phone out and check the time to confirm the rumble I'm suddenly hearing this late afternoon. The bitumen seemingly shaking with the bus's chugging climb and I curse myself for forgetting to mind the time.

I stop mid-stride and do an almost comical look to the left and right of me. There's nowhere to hide except our neighbour's low stone wall where a willow tree's lazy branches hang like a curtain in the front garden to provide some extra cover. I resignedly perch on the wall, unwrap the parka from around my waist and shrug it on, flipping the hood up. I burrow my hands into the pockets and try to fold my body into obscurity as I listen to the well-worn spiel of my family history coming from the booming microphone like a demented real-time Wikipedia entry.

'Folks, we're at the top of the hill and the cream of the crop, with this next destination – the historic Lovinger House, home to the Famous Lovinger Theatrical Family . . .'

Secreted deep in my parka's hood, nobody can see me mouth along with the tour guide's next words:

'. . . some of whom still reside here – *to this day*!'

I roll my eyes.

None of the tourists even spare me a glance; they're completely riveted to the wrought-iron gates and clouds of bougainvillea climbing the high stone walls. The gentleman with a microphone standing at the front of the bus begins the rundown.

It's not easy to compress a couple of centuries' worth of family and film history into a tour-bus pit stop that doesn't cause traffic congestion on this moneyed street. But the tour guide talks fast and gives a concise history, which even I can admit is pretty impressive.

He begins with the Lovinger who was tried and convicted of highway robbery in London and who came over to Hobart Town on the *Minerva* in 1818. His son would eventually go on to create a successful touring Bushranger Show of his father's exploits, greatly exaggerated.

This of course leads into the legend of John Lovinger, who played a terrifically over-the-top death scene as Ned Kelly in the world's first ever feature-length narrative movie, *The Story of the Kelly Gang* in 1906. That we had a real-life highwayman on our family tree surely helped all of the Lovingers keep getting dastardly and daring roles (the tour guide's words, not mine) throughout their careers.

This seamless segue leads into talking about the next notable Lovinger and one who had a long-running feud throughout the Golden Age of Hollywood against fellow Tasmanian actor – and here I reflexively curl my lip at the tour guide's reveal – Errol Flynn.

Adam Lovinger competed against the swashbuckler for *Captain Blood* in 1935 right through to *The Adventures of Robin Hood* in 1938, always missing out – but that all changed when he nabbed the role of Lancelot in the 1939 Warner Bros big-budget movie *Lancelot of the Lake.*

What the man behind the microphone doesn't know to note is that it's also a point of extreme pride in the family that Adam eventually got a statue in 1959 for Best Supporting Actor in *Son of Reprieve,* while Errol never got a thing. But I recommend never asking a Lovinger descendant to go any deeper into the great Errol Flynn feud and especially don't mention that Errol got a reserve named after him, along the northern end of the Marieville Esplanade at Sandy Bay. It's a point of serious contention in the family, and one we're constantly complaining about to the Hobart City Council, I can assure you.

I don't pipe up about any of this, of course. I just continue to sit and hide in plain sight on the low stone wall, guesstimating that there's one more subject to be covered before the bus will pull away from my front gate.

'Folks, that brings us to the most infamous, and current occupant of the house, Lottie Lovinger!' Here to aid the finale, the guide turns around and presses a button on an old-school CD player behind him that starts crackling out some eerie music, which I've always assumed is somehow related to *The Hazards* franchise.

Sure enough, he starts up again. 'Lottie Lovinger got her big break at age 19, playing cricket-bat-wielding, short-short-wearing Hannah-Jane in Sydney-based Drummoyne House Studios' slasher film franchise, *The Hazards.* The role rocketed Lottie onto the world stage to finally follow in her famous family's footsteps, and also led the charge for a new kind of schlock-horror cinema both here and in America throughout the 1960s and 70s!'

I go very still after this factoid, because I know the next bullet point that's coming, and I refuse to let it visibly hit me.

'Lottie returned to her horror roots with her granddaughter in the Oz indie hit *Blood & Jacaranda* that sparked a revival of Lottie's career, and even saw her nab a star on the Hollywood Walk of Fame!'

I don't know if he says anything else. The static on the microphone and the tinny sound of the music seem to be echoing in my brain and I have to force myself to breathe deeply – in through my nose, and out through my mouth – as people start snapping photos on their phones from where they sit atop the bus.

Though I really don't know why they bother.

There's nothing to see at Lovinger House from their vantage point. They can't peek at the beautiful gardens from the pavement, through the thick bougainvillea growing like a purple cloud along the high brick fence-line. Maybe they can just glimpse the tops of our dormer roof, and the railed widow's walk in the middle, where a Unitron-model telescope sits throughout summer.

But they will not see the thick, wooden front door with metal lattice, arched like something out of a medieval castle – nor the brass doorknocker in the shape of a thylacine head. They can't even spy the north-facing conservatory with checkerboard tile, where an old leather Chesterfield sits facing the overgrown garden – a memento from the set of a McDonagh Sisters film, *Those Who Love.* And they definitely can't see the Corinthian-style columns and balustraded terrace that opens out from the library directly above.

And as the bus pulls out and keeps lumbering along, the tourists don't even notice when a real-life Lovinger slips between the heavy wrought-iron gates and jogs her way up the winding white-gravel driveway, trying to beat a sun-shower that just broke through. She runs quickly past the weeping Japanese maples, bleeding red for spring.

There really is nothing for them to see here.

FOUR

I'm leaving puddles.

The parka was too thin to save me from the sudden Hobart shower, and now that I'm standing in our long entryway by the staircase, I find that I am dripping on the star-burst black and yellow Art Deco tiles.

'You cannot be serious!'

For a second I think it might be a reprimand for the mess but then I realise my mum's exclamation has come from the kitchen at the back of the house. The hallway and the entrance are like a wind-tunnel carrying her anxious voice so clearly that I shake myself, spraying droplets everywhere. I peel my parka off and hang it from one of the tarnished brass hooks on the wall, the ones shaped like tiger paws. Then I toe off my Converse shoes and squelch my way down the hall in damp socks, leaving a faint outline of my feet as I go.

'Kaleb, Kaleb – please don't do this, whatever else happened you and Lottie have . . .'

My mum is sitting at the kitchen counter with a hand to her forehead and her mobile phone pressed to her ear. I can just make out the muffled voice of one of my ex-grandfathers on the other end.

'She would be there for you! I can promise you that, she would be there at your side if you were in her shoes, but you won't even afford her the dignity of –'

The sound of a dial tone is as loud as my heartbeat and I watch as my mother pulls the phone back from her ear and stares at the empty screen for a long second. It's then that I clear my throat. She jumps a little in her seat, clasps her phone to her chest, closes her eyes and lets out a deep sigh. 'Ellie, you scared the life out of me!' Then she opens her eyes again and peppers questions at me. 'How is she? No change? Jasper got there okay?'

'Fine, no change, and Jasper is there now,' I answer each in turn.

Then her eyes widen as she really takes me in. 'Did you walk home from the hospital? Ellie, it's getting colder in the evenings – you'll catch your death!'

That marks two interesting idioms she's now used in a row, considering where I've just come from.

'It's fine. I felt like walking,' I say, moving to the fridge to stare at its contents before gently closing the door, realising I'm not hungry after all.

'So – how is Kaleb?' I ask, turning back around.

My mum lets out another deep sigh. 'Don't ask. He's refusing to come down and see her, and has also told us not to expect him for the funeral . . .'

I can't say I'm shocked. Kaleb was Lottie's third husband, who left her when he found out she'd cheated on him with a

Neighbours series regular, during a ten-episode guest-arc she did back in the early-00s.

But I don't say anything. Instead I lean against the counter and take in all the paperwork surrounding my mother. 'What's this?'

She peers at me over the reading glasses she's just slipped on, perching them at the end of her nose. 'Preparations,' she says, 'and communications – I'm trying to find everyone's phone numbers or their agent's details, or friends-of-friends who might be able to track them down for me.'

Oh – *right* – Lottie's final concerns that we're all trying to ease.

I frown down at the many planners, envelopes, scraps of paper and old-school address books from back in the days when people didn't have a contacts app on their phone, or social media to keep track of everyone. There's clearly an added difficulty on display here, of dealing with mostly famous people who are prone to privacy anyway, coupled with the majority of them being from an analogue generation when it comes to communication.

Part of me is comforted by the amount of debris, the clear evidence that still exists of work to be done . . . as though Lottie will conveniently wait for us to finish all these provisions. Like all of this is evidence that we – that *I* – still have time, like maybe it's not lost entirely.

Thinking of that has my mind buzzing again, and, like before, I force myself to breathe in through my nose and out through my mouth. On an exhale I ask Mum, 'So, how's it going anyway?'

'Well, doing all of this under a veil of secrecy isn't helping, and your *bubbe* burnt a few bridges in her time,' she says.

Lottie's wishes on her end-of-life care have always been well known and made clear among the family, and especially to my mother – her eldest child and only daughter. Acknowledgement of a future end and final curtain call is just expected when you have somewhat of a 'legacy' to be upheld, and Lottie has always made it apparent that however her finale comes, she wants it kept private.

She wants friends and family to be there, but for the general public – and media especially – to be kept out of her end-of-life affairs, such as they are. Mum and the uncles are interpreting that to mean that in Lottie's current circumstances friends and relatives should begin saying their goodbyes but there's to be a complete media blackout otherwise.

This is proving tricky when your family is as big as ours, and you tend to have reclusive friends on multiple continents, but Mum's also right. Lottie burnt bridges in her time – and now we're all left to sift through the ashes.

Which is pretty hard, when you're also one of the embers.

I can see Mum is probably having the exact same thought because now she's taking off her glasses and really looking at me.

'Did you talk to her, Ellie?'

She looks tired. I'm pretty sure she's still on London time, her internal clock hasn't properly aligned, and taking turns going to the hospital and sitting by Lottie's bedside at all hours of the night and day can't be helping. I'm also pretty sure that her worrying about how I'm coping with being home and in Lottie's vicinity isn't making the situation any easier. So I fall into old habits and deflect by changing the subject.

'Hey, guess what came on TMC right before I left?' Before she can answer, I say, '*Seven Hills.*'

My mum's face breaks into the first genuine smile I've seen since I got here.

'Oh, you were *obsessed* with that movie when you were younger!' She gives a little chuckle. 'The one time my mother did babysitting duty was whenever that movie was on TV, and I could just plonk you in front of the telly and you'd sit quietly for the whole two hours . . .' She sighs again, 'And then we busted that DVD of it because you watched it so many times that it started skipping.'

'I remember.'

'Oh, and how you used to wave at her!' Mum's smile is getting a little watery now, and then she looks at me and frowns. 'You were obsessed with her once upon a time, kiddo. She was one of your favourite people.'

I remember that too.

But I am not ready to reminisce, so I fake a yawn and tell Mum I should go for a warm soak in the claw-foot tub upstairs if I want to avoid catching cold.

But before I leave, I wave a hand at the paper debris surrounding her and ask if there's anything else I can help with.

'Actually,' Mum says, and stretches her arm out to the end of the island and hands me a bundle of envelopes of various sizes, wrapped in twine – actual, honest-to-goodness twine, like we're back in 1890.

'These arrived – some of Lottie's fan mail for this month . . .'

Like clockwork, Lottie's agents have sent through her regular mail delivery. They're practically family anyway, having been with Lottie since she was a teenager, but her Sydney agency have now become an integral part of the current process of fulfilling Lottie's last wishes.

So far the agents are helping us go to extraordinary lengths to keep everything quiet. They even put out an official press release about her retirement due to health reasons from a stage production she was meant to be debuting in later this month. It was a little light on truth and relied heavily on the age-old swollen lymph nodes escape route.

I wonder why they can't handle the fan mail side of things too? And I ask as much.

'Oh no, the agents are adamant that Lottie always dealt with fan mail herself. "Gave it a personal touch," according to them. I checked, and you'll find a stack of signed headshots in the office cabinet upstairs, and if you want to pen an additional note – feel free to. There's prepaid stamped envelopes in one of the drawers too.'

I nod once and clutch the mail to my chest. I'm heading towards the door but not before Mum reminds me once more, what I'm really doing here.

'Ellie – it's okay if you don't know what to say to her.' She gives me a small, encouraging smile. 'I honestly think that after everything, it's enough that you're even here.'

FIVE

The next morning, I come to stand in front of the two framed photos that hang right outside the bedroom of the blue room on the second floor where I'm staying.

The originals are side-by-side at ACMI – that's, the Australian Centre for the Moving Image in Melbourne. And those two are signed – one has Lottie's signature in silver ink, all looped and precise in the bottom right corner. The other has my best attempt at proper penmanship, *Ellie Marsden*, tucked away at the bottom left in a hard-to-see blue ink.

These ones at Lovinger House hanging on the red mahogany panelling of the hallway are just copies.

I honestly don't even remember where or when the first photo was taken. Lottie's not in costume yet; she's standing up, her hands gesturing in the air as she's running lines in her trailer. I think I was about six or seven, so checking her IMDb puts her in one of the failed Australian sitcoms, or that Hallmark Christmas movie that she shot on the Sunshine Coast.

The *where* and *when* doesn't really matter though, because she's out of focus in the mirror anyway. My dad took the first photo – and he was taking it of me. He was standing behind me, and you can just see the cuff of his shirt sleeve and the edge of his vintage Canon camera in the mirror. I'm sitting at Lottie's vanity, one of those with little lightbulbs lining the edge of the mirror. My elbows are on her dresser, chin in my hands as I watch her run those lines, and my reflection in the mirror looks very focused and serious like I'm studying her.

The second photo is more famous, you've no doubt seen it. A photographer and a journalist came on set for two days to do a story about a little movie filming in Adelaide, called *Blood & Jacaranda*. It was only an article for a local magazine, but I hear the photographer made a fair bit of money from selling that photo to bigger outlets since.

In the photo, I'm eleven years old and sitting in front of a much bigger mirror in the special-effects trailer, taking a break between make-up and prosthetics. Lottie is behind me leaning in the doorway with her arms crossed, and this time it's she who is concentrating and studying – taking in the two halves of my face.

One side is flushed with a rosy cheek but otherwise untouched. On the other side, however, my left eye is dead with a cloudy white contact, and there's deep latex claw-marks made to look like they've hit bone on my cheek. My hair was longer then and they used gel to make it look wet and tangled. But what's really striking is that with the two of us framed in the mirror, my hair colour and Lottie's deep-auburn colour look similar to the synthetic blood they've used in the fake cuts.

I remember after shooting I begged Mum to let me cut my hair off. I wanted a pixie cut even though I didn't really know what that meant. I just knew I didn't want to look like me anymore.

Come to think of it – maybe I didn't want to look like her either.

And it's amusing to me, that in a house with eleven bedrooms, one permanently Lottie's and two currently occupied by Mum and Jasper respectively, that still leaves eight to choose from and I gravitated to my old one where I have to pass Lottie and the old me every day in the hallway.

I am pulled back into the present by the sound of the front door opening and closing down below, which makes me frown because I didn't think it was changeover yet, my turn to tap back in at the hospital. Though I wouldn't be surprised if I'd lost track of time. These first few days being home and settling into hospital rhythms feels like we're in a time-vacuum, where days stretch and contract at random, and hours bleed into one another or else vanish entirely. It's a kind of permanent, emotional jetlag we're all adjusting to.

I hold onto the chunky polished balustrade as I descend the stairs, and see Mum at the entryway, hanging her scarf and throwing her keys into an antique glass bowl that sits on the sideboard.

'Ellie, morning!' she says, 'What are you doing up so early?'

Right on time the grandfather clock that sits beneath the stairs chimes that it's 6 a.m. I watch as Mum pushes open the sliding barn doors that lead into the front sitting room and goes marching in.

I finish my descent and follow her. 'Is it my turn? You didn't message me. I can head down now . . .'

'No, that's okay.' Mum slings her handbag onto the frayed teal fainting couch in front of the cold fireplace, and then dramatically takes a seat there too before she drops the bombshell. 'Poe arrived early this morning; he's there now.'

I stop at the entrance to the sitting room, my socked feet on the carpeted edge. 'What?!'

'He bought a one-way ticket from Auckland, so – I guess he's intending to stay for a bit.'

I have so many questions running through my mind, but I grasp for just one. 'Where is he staying?'

'I don't know. At the Grand Chancellor maybe?'

'Mum!'

'What?'

'There are seven bedrooms to choose from. You could leave him the entire third floor if you wanted to. Don't be ridiculous.'

'We could have a lot of family coming over in the next few days and weeks . . .'

'Poe *is* family!'

I can see it's on the tip of Mum's tongue to debate this, but I won't hear a word against him, let alone any insinuations that he's not Lovinger enough to stay here.

But Poe is to Mum what Lottie is to me – a sore point.

No doubt you already know that my mum is the only child of Harvey Hutton, Lottie's first husband. Harvey died at the age of 27. He's become one of those tragic stars better known for what they *could* have been than the scant filmography they left behind. In Harvey's case he did a handful of bit parts on TV, and then a breakout role in the adaptation of *The Harp in the South* in 1969, around the same time he met Lottie. He had an Oscar-nominated turn as a corrupt police-officer in *Tender* – and then he died when my mum was really young.

Poe and Lottie married six months later.

And even though they were long divorced by the time I came along, Poe is still my favourite of the grandfathers, much to my mum's chagrin.

Admittedly, I never met Harvey; Kaleb and Lottie's relationship was always stormy, and by the time Shane came into the family I was old enough to be embarrassed by my grandmother's collection of husbands. It's also that Poe and Lottie had the best post-divorce relationship of all her exes, and he's just always been there – for family birthdays and get-togethers, long weekends and every Rosh Hashanah. Even Kaleb and Shane were happy to have him around and kept in touch with him long after they'd ceased communication with Lottie directly, speaking to her only via lawyers or family intermediaries. This is also pretty incredible considering Kaleb and Shane had three sons between them with Lottie: my mum's half-brothers Jasper, Tobin and Seth.

But of all of them, Poe is my favourite. He has no children, and while Poe always considered my mum to be his daughter, she never felt the same way. It's long been a sore point in our family among many open wounds and Mum has never been too thrilled with my clear choice of Poe as preferred grandparent.

Mention of and interaction with him makes my mum revert to her brattier youth – like right now.

'Fine, you can invite him to stay when you go down later in the day,' she all but huffs.

'Thank you.'

But as I turn to leave, she feels the need to add something.

'I just don't know how thrilled Lottie would be with the idea of him being here.'

I turn back around. 'What do you mean? They're best friends. I'm only surprised he wasn't here earlier.'

Mum sits up straight and starts unwinding the messy bun that sits atop her head. Her hair is the same colour as mine and Lottie's – deep blood red, though with streaks of grey now that she's not bothered by it enough to dye it.

'Ellie,' she sighs and lets her hands drop as her hair shakes loose. 'There's a lot you've missed out on and I haven't told you about while you were . . .' she rotates her hand in the air, searching for the word, 'taking an extended break from the family.'

I don't say anything.

'Never mind, it's fine,' she says.

'You do know that Poe and I keep in touch – all the time?' I say, maybe a bit defensively because while it's true Poe and I have talked on the phone almost every week since I started boarding school in Melbourne, he respected my wish for distance from the family, and I haven't actually *seen* him for three years either.

'I know, but I also don't know how much he will have told you, since . . .'

'Since what?' I fold my arms across my chest and wait for her reply.

'Since Lottie asked him not to.'

SIX

I'm still thinking of Mum's words – her warning, really – when I arrive at the Creswell Hospital just after noon.

It's officially the last day of September and even though there's a slight bite of cold in the air and the skies are grey on this Monday, there's also colour to be found everywhere. I even walked through St David's Park on the way, just to see the blackwood trees aflame.

Turner Classic Movies is still playing on the TV, and without even craning my neck to see, I can tell from the sound that it's *Casablanca* – a Poe favourite.

He must feel my presence because he lifts his head and smiles. He manages to not look the least bit surprised when I walk into the room, and say, 'What in heaven's name brought you to Tasmania?'

Without missing a beat, he replies, 'My health. I came to Tasmania for the waters.'

'The waters? What waters? We're . . .' I shrug, and break character. 'Actually, this whole bit doesn't work so well when we're on a literal island.'

He stands, and still says the *Casablanca* line we're both reaching for: 'I was misinformed.'

And then I'm moving forward and bear-hugging him fiercely, breathing in his home smell of lemon for the trees, and tobacco for the habit, still faintly there even beneath the stink of airplane travel.

We pull apart so he can get a better look at me, and I can see how tired he is – and not just the kind of tired that comes from being 78 years old either.

'Hi, kiddo,' Poe says. 'You got so tall.'

I immediately start crying, and so he gently rests his forehead against mine, our noses touching briefly, a gentle *hongi*, which Poe once told me during bedtime stories was a tradition of sharing the breath of life given by the gods, going back to when Tāne created Hineahuone.

And then we're apart again and he's cupping my face in his hands, brushing my tears away with the pads of his thumbs.

I shake myself a little and his hands fall to his sides, then in sync we both turn to Lottie lying prone in bed. Her chest is rising and falling steadily still.

I sniff and ask, 'Has she woken up?'

Poe shuffles back to the wing chair and takes a seat, lifting her right hand again and cradling it in both of his, the position I found him in. 'Briefly, when they came to dress her and give more morphine. But her eyes weren't focused. I don't think she knew it was me.'

I nod once. 'I keep missing her.'

I go to pull over the extra visitor chair by the door and take a seat on her other side – but unlike Poe I won't touch her.

'When did Mum tell you?' I ask, and instantly Poe's face reveals all.

'Your dad did, actually. He called me a couple of days ago.'

I feel my face heating up, at the same time my heart swells and I have to bite my fingernails into my palms to fight the pain of missing my dad so much. Even when he's not here, he's playing peacekeeper and director, gently pulling strings and making sure we're all where we need to be.

'I'm so sorry. I should have reached out. I didn't even think . . .'

Poe waves my apology away. 'Hey, hey – it's okay! You had a lot on your mind, you and Louise both did, and Michael knew that.'

Michael, my dad. Sometimes I think I gravitated to Poe so much because he and my dad seem so alike; these gentle giants who observe a lot but say very little, and surprise you with the amount of detail they retain. It's also another reason I can never understand why my mum resists Poe so much but is head-over-heels still in love with my dad's same countenance.

And then I guiltily think back to Mum sitting at the kitchen island, all those pieces of paper spread out around her as she goes on an expedition to track down family and friends. I don't think telling Poe will help anything though, and so I don't. Instead I nod at his big blue suitcase sitting in the corner of the room. Clearly, he came here straight from the airport.

'I don't know if Mum mentioned anything, but she's insisting you come and stay with us.'

'Is she now?'

I keep a completely straight face. 'Of course, we need you – and Lottie would want you with us.'

Poe looks down at her hand, which he's still gently clutching in his, and I clear my throat to ask him something. 'When did you two last talk?'

He shrugs. 'A couple of weeks? I was going to come down for her first show at the Theatre Royal, take her out to dinner and celebrate – or else whisk her away, maybe home with me for a mini-break.' He looks up at me then.

He means the theatre production she was meant to star in – *The Lion's Bride* – a limited-run, four-days a week and her celebrated return to the boards after so long gone to film and television.

'And did she seem okay?' I ask.

He nods again. 'Fine, happy even. She said it felt good to be busy again.'

Nothing out of the ordinary, despite my mum's warning.

'And so it's settled – you'll come to the house?' Poe still looks unsure, so I make a different appeal. 'Besides, if anyone sees you at the Hotel Grand Chancellor and realises the great Poe Tuhana is in town, they might start connecting dots with Lottie who is supposed to be "in recovery".'

Poe may have had the bad luck to fall in love with an actor, but that was never his arena. He's a costume designer, and an award-winning one at that. He's won a BAFTA, two Oscars, GOFTA, Golden Globe, AACTA and a whole lot more. But his marriage to Lottie, coming so soon on the heels of his best friend Harvey Hutton's death – and a divorce years later – does mean he's been in the spotlight and gossip pages a fair bit.

It probably also helps that he's been blessed with the kind of face you could put on a bottle of salad dressing to sell millions.

Even now, approaching 80, his curly salt-and-pepper hair and stubbled beard have only given him more of an air of the debonair.

'Okay, I'll stay,' Poe says, just as Captain Renault is explaining to Ilsa that Rick Blaine is the kind of man that he'd fall in love with, if he were a woman.

SEVEN

It's three nights later before we're all together for the first time, at the same time.

An old actor friend of Lottie's has flown into town, and offered to stay with her overnight – in fact, she insisted upon it. (And if I was one to name-drop, which I am not, I could impress upon you how much you don't feel inclined to say 'no' to this person, especially when they've set aside their busy schedule of activism and protesting at the United States Capitol in Washington, D.C. to come say goodbye to one of their best and most beloved friends.)

So with our marching orders, we all decided to sit down for dinner and have our first proper home-cooked meal – Poe's tuna lasagne extravaganza (which just means three types of cheese).

Me, Jasper, Mum and Poe are all sitting around the formal dining room just off the kitchen, at our large oak dining table. It can seat twenty in a pinch, so we're all crowded down one end with Mum at the head. She's sitting in one of the two original high-backed chairs from the round table of *Lancelot of the Lake*, reupholstered many times since 1939.

At least, we were sitting – until Mum and I got a phone call from Dad, and had to briefly duck into the butler's pantry to talk to him on the old-style rotary wall phone that hangs in there.

Jasper and Poe waited for us, chatting quietly while we updated Dad, and now we're back and the lasagne is slightly colder, as the conversation turns chilly too.

'Louise, how's Michael?' Poe asks, innocently enough.

'He's fine, but of course you knew that already – since you spoke to him recently.'

Yes. A small jab aimed at both Poe and my dad that leaves the table slightly uncomfortable.

I feel the need to add for Jasper's benefit, 'He can't leave the production right now, or this month so he might not even make it for the . . .' I was going to say funeral or service, but it's inappropriate, so I leave the sentence unfinished.

Mum throws Poe a mean side-eye before reaching over and gently tapping me on the wrist, until I look at her. 'Hey, not your dad's fault – okay?'

'Yeah, I know.'

'I mean it, kiddo. They've got him chained to his contract. The whole production has been built around him and if he steps away and ticket sales slump, they lose their investors and nail him for breach of contract.'

Dad is a director. He works in theatre. Very specifically, he works in Shakespearean theatre, and even more specifically he works in modern impressionist interpretations of the Bard. He's kind of like Kenneth Branagh and has worked with him too except he's nowhere near as famous, only in certain circles. He's currently putting on a production of a gender-flipped and heavily

Brexit-inspired *Macbeth* at the West End that's getting rave-to-middling reviews so he can't up and leave while the company tries to get more bums on seats. It's also that his suddenly stepping away from such a big production to return to Australia might raise suspicions about the health of his famous mother-in-law. And so, the subterfuge continues and Dad is locked in Britain.

I envy those people who can walk into a cinema or theatre and just enjoy the spectacle for a few hours. I've never had that luxury. Instead, I grew up knowing exactly how the sausage gets made and how much it costs to make it. But even with all the logic gained from living behind the velvet curtain, I can't help feeling a little bit of resentment towards Dad for not being here when we need him.

Before he got pulled to the West End, my dad had regular Shakespearean seasons as the artistic director of the Hobart Children's Theatre Company. I was awed by the idea of dressing up and getting clapped for playing make-believe with other people's words, alongside kids who loved it all as much as I did. And when I was just seven years old I begged and begged to be allowed to audition. When my parents gave me the all-clear, I threw my whole body into rehearsing and practising to the point that even now I can recite Puck's 'If we shadows have offended' from *A Midsummer Night's Dream* in my sleep.

Lottie didn't help me. I can't remember even asking her to or if my parents told her not to interfere. But I enjoyed my own company, figuring out the words and what every moment of them meant in the privacy of our vast library . . .

No, Lottie didn't help me. But I do remember the moment I crossed my legs at the ankle and slowly folded into sitting cross-legged on the cold wooden boards of the Theatre Royal stage, reciting the lines 'give me your hands, if we be friends, and Robin shall restore amends' – and then laying my hands palm up on my knees. I gave a small smile to the audience of three directors and teachers from the company, sitting in the darkened middle row I had to project to.

And then I realised there had been four people in the audience – as Lottie rose and started clapping in a standing ovation.

I hadn't known she'd been there. Not even my dad was allowed to sit in on the audition but somehow she'd snuck in to the back row. And even now I can hear the sound of her whooping and cheering, the jangle of her bracelets, the clapped cacophony echoing around the walls of that epic theatre.

And I was accepted, and I did love playing make-believe – for a time.

'Of course, that's completely understandable,' Poe says, breaking my memories apart and bringing me back to the moment.

It's Jasper who takes the next conversational plunge.

'Yael's coming for the weekend,' he says, and I sputter slightly as the sip of water I just took goes down the wrong way.

Mum puts her fork down to slap me on the back. 'Oh, that's good of her!' she says.

'Yes, she can't take too much time off. First year at The University of Sydney is very demanding, but she wants to be here while she can.'

'Ellie, it'll be nice that you'll have a bit of company and not have to hang around with us oldies!'

'Yeah, if there's time we could definitely do something – small, during the day . . . She'll probably want to be at the hospital though, so there's no pressure . . .' I can't help rambling since Jasper has caught me slightly off-guard. I honestly thought I'd have more time before having to choose how to feel about seeing Yael again for the first time since I was 14.

I can tell from Poe's hidden smirk that I'm not doing a great job of keeping my cool.

'Honey, I think while Yael's here it'd be good for you to get out of the house and hospital for a bit – let your hair down, maybe?' Mum says.

I'm nodding down at my plate, not wanting to look anyone in the eye in case they see the horror in mine at the very thought of letting my hair down with Yael, of all people.

'Yael could use a little break too. She's sailed through her first year at The University of Sydney but I think a little time to unwind could do her good.'

I wonder if Jasper gets a reduction in tuition every time he name-checks the University.

'I know you don't have the same pressures, Ellie, since you finished school but maybe you and Yael could talk options, hear what she has to say about The University of Sydney as a pathway for you.'

I don't know – maybe he has stock options in the place?

'That is, if you know what you want to do, Ellie?'

I do not. I'm 17 and graduated as of late last month. It's a long and boring recitation, but having lived in London for a time, the Teaching Powers That Be deemed I'd come out one year ahead of my Australian studies, so I moved up a grade when

I began boarding school. Throw in some advanced subjects and mid-year exams and I've effectively been an early graduate as of mid-September, and completely without purpose ever since.

'I'm still weighing up my options,' I say. And then Poe saves me by prompting Jasper to give a full run-down of how Yael's first year has gone.

'Which university is she at again?' he asks.

EIGHT

Air is my first instinct when I suddenly realise that I need it.

I flail awake on an inward breath that turns into an oxygen-deprived snort and discover Yael beside me in bed, her thumb and index finger hovering above my head, pinching my nose.

'The prodigal granddaughter has returned, and she snores,' she says.

I reply by rolling away from her and onto my side. I pull up the blanket over my head but she yanks it down again just as quickly.

'Get up. I'm bored.'

I sigh and roll onto my back, stare up at the white ceiling rose above my head and silently count to ten. And the whole time Yael just stares at me, lying on her side with her head in her hand patiently waiting for me to gain patience.

'Good morning, Yael. When did you arrive?' I finally ask.

'About two hours ago, and Aunt Louise has already informed me that you're keen to attend a party tonight.'

I sit up and put my back against the dark blue velvet headboard. I pull the blankets up with me so Yael can't see I'm wearing a *She-Ra and the Princesses of Power* pyjama top.

'You've been misinformed,' I finally say, which makes Yael flop onto her back and laugh.

'Oh, Ellie – you never change,' then she's rolling off the bed and standing, hands on hips and her head cocked as she looks at me, 'except that you lost that British accent, *finally*!'

'I wasn't there long enough to get an accent.'

'Oh – but you did! You sounded like Keanu Reeves in *Dracula*. It was horrendous,' she says, elongating the last word into something far more pompous.

My cousin said something similar the last time we saw each other during our first visit home after leaving for England when I was 14. Mum had been gently encouraging me to heal old wounds and reconnect with the family, so she insisted on us returning home to Hobart for a little holiday. At Lovinger House, I gorged myself on honey-dipped apples to celebrate Rosh Hashanah – the New Year. Lottie and Poe played hosts, Yael was here with her parents and I stayed in this very same blue room and it almost felt like old times. To the point that Yael snuck in here one night and I woke, much as now, to feel her looming over me. 'So does this mean you're back to normal?' she'd asked.

I'd been groggy, and I rolled over in a huff and asked what she was on about.

I could feel her eyes rolling in the dark. 'With your tantrum and punishing Lottie – are you finally over it?

My face had gone hot and my heart sped up. I'd often wondered how much Yael knew, since I hadn't wanted to tell her. And now I had some idea of what the rest of the family must have thought of mine and my parents' fight with Lottie, that was only starting to heal, and slowly.

'You don't know what you're talking about,' I stammered, still turned away from her and trying to control the hammering of my heart.

Yael had flopped onto her back then and laughed. 'It's actually hilarious that you say you're over acting and everything, because you've been putting it on all weekend. Right down to that Madonna-fake British accent . . .' she said, her voice dripping with sarcasm.

I don't remember falling asleep or Yael finally leaving – just an almighty row the next morning when I accused Lottie of turning the family against me. I called her a liar and an actor – which, I screamed, was the same thing – and I said I never wanted to see her again. And I didn't, for a time.

Even when my parents thought it was better for me to return to Australia, I refused to live in Tasmania so boarding school in Melbourne was the compromise. And I suppose a small part of me also thought that boarding school sounded terribly exciting – at least based on my love of stories set in such places. I thought it'd be a cross between the Jellicoe School of Melina Marchetta's *On the Jellicoe Road* and Larwood House from Diana Wynne Jones' *Witch Week*. Maybe with less magic and factional infighting because I'd had more than enough of both within my own family.

The memories fade and now I watch present-day Yael as she saunters around the blue room, making her way over to the antique dressing table and vanity against the far wall. It looks like something Carol Brady would sit in front of, with five tall, curved mirrored panels arranged vaguely in the shape of a clamshell, two round drawers on either side and then a little cut-out section in the middle to sit down on a dainty blue upholstered chair.

Yael briefly lifts up the packet of Lottie's fan mail I still haven't gone through, then puts it down again and takes a seat. She starts opening and closing the drawers until she finds the one containing costume jewellery and begins holding gaudy earrings up against her head.

The thing is Yael could pull off wearing any of them. Even the chunky fake-gold elephant clip-on earrings with amethyst stones in the eyes. Because Yael is out-and-out gorgeous.

Jasper and my aunt Constance adopted her as a baby. She's 18 months older than me. We also went to the same school for a time. Not that we ever ran in the same circles. Age difference aside, Yael operates on a completely different frequency to me, and always has. So much so that it's hard to remember a time when she used to sleep over at Lovinger House in this very room with me, and we'd do exactly what she is now doing – go through all the drawers, cupboards, and closets and pull out decades of abundance in quality dress-up gear and then go sauntering around the house looking like ladies who brunch.

There are plenty of photos of us from this time – taken at our insistence, posing at the top of the stairs – me with a scowl on my face, my dark red locks normally in pigtails, and Yael with her perfect smile, green eyes and cascade of tightly-coiled black curls.

Nothing much has changed except for my lopped-off hair, which is now more like a red shag than pixie cut and emphasises even more that Yael wears all the glamour in our family.

'So Uncle Tobin and Seth will be here in the next few days,' Yael says, head down and still rifling through the jewellery drawer. 'Any idea when the Queensland cousins are coming?'

Yael could be speaking about a family reunion, or an upcoming birthday celebration for all her deliberate talking around the subject of what's coming. But it's not disinterest or delusion; it's care and consideration. We don't talk about funerals and what comes after when someone is still with us, and has not yet died. Instead and when we can, we talk in euphemisms, taking care to verbally pussyfoot around the topic . . . Yael is asking if the cousins have been called home yet, because the funeral might happen sooner than we think.

And all I can think to say is, 'They'll come when they need to.'

The second the words are out, the room suddenly feels colder. Because I don't know the answer to the question she's really asking. And just thinking on the processes and steps that will come next feels too big and sad a task.

As if she can hear the thought turning over in my mind, Yael catches my eye in one of the clamshell panels of the vanity mirror, and I wonder if we're thinking the same thing. It's like we're tempting fate or willing the moment to come, even if we don't say any of this out loud.

It's almost comforting then, to think Yael feels as overwhelmed as I do.

She turns around and rests her chin on the back of the chair. Looking at me she asks, 'What's she like, anyway?'

'What do you mean?'

'How does she look? What's it like to see her, like that?'

Now the room feels too hot, and I push the blankets off me and huff, 'You're the medical student, shouldn't you know?'

'I'm a first year; it's all textbooks and theory.' Yael rolls her eyes and sits up, glaring at me. 'Just – tell me. What am I in for?'

'She's . . . sleeping. Basically. She's on a lot of morphine to manage her pain, and they're feeding her via a tube in her stomach. They don't think she's feeling much of anything but she could come out of it at any moment. Though they highly doubt it,' I shrug. 'Apparently, she wakes up now and then when the morphine wears off, but I haven't seen her like that since I've been here.'

Yael's face has paled since I started talking, so I shrug again and try to end on something positive. 'But she looks – you know – peaceful or whatever.'

She gets up from the vanity and walks back around to the opposite side of my bed. She lies down beside me again, on top of the covers with her back against the headboard too. She crosses her socked feet at the ankle and her upper arm gently touches mine. 'It was weird arriving here, without her,' she says.

'I know.'

'There should have been a Kate Ceberano song blasting from the library speakers, and she should have been at the top of the stairs in something flowing and fabulous, greeting me by announcing that I'd give Dorothy Dandridge and Diahann Carroll a run for their money.'

I loll my head to the side and stare at her, until Yael acknowledges me and throws her hands up briefly. 'What? I loved that she appealed to my vanity!'

We don't say anything for a bit. And just when I think I should reach over and take her hand, tell her that maybe I have missed her, and us, and this – just talking and being quiet together. But then she abruptly changes the subject, looping back around to the idea of attending a party tonight.

'It's Friday, I've been back in Hobart for two hours and I've already been invited to two parties – and you *clearly* need to get out, so you're coming to at least one of them with me!'

'We don't have to do this,' I say, and gesture between us with one hand. 'We could even just say that we went to a party together, and instead you can drop me off at Constitution Dock and I'll grab some fish 'n' chips, then you swing by on your way home and collect me?'

Even as I say it, I'm watching Yael sit up and slowly turn her horrified face fully towards me. 'Are you serious?'

'Serious as a stroke.'

'Can you just get over yourself for one night?'

'What?'

'I know you hate all of us, and what you think we did to you – but we didn't choose sides, Ellie . . . you just didn't stick around long enough to see.'

That stings. And I want to bring up the fact that the last time we were in this room, she'd accused me of faking my hurt over incidents she clearly didn't have any idea about. But I'm too tired, and I wouldn't know where to start. I feel like I should have rehearsed explaining my side of events and getting her to understand, but instead I've missed my cue and forgotten my lines.

'I don't hate you,' I say instead, but even to my ears I sound unconvincing, and of course Yael rolls her eyes.

'You're not as good an actor as they say you are.'

There's complete silence after Yael says this. For my part I can't believe she almost perfectly echoed my thoughts. And then I let out a giant huff, followed by, 'You *really* just said that!'

And then we're both laughing. It's genuine at first, deep-bellied and building, but then it tapers off and we're both left staring at each other.

'Okay, I'll go with you,' I finally say, because that feels like it could be a good place to start figuring out my part and what I want to say, what I need Yael to know.

'Thank you.'

'But I'm not going to have a good time.'

NINE

We're hurtling over a bridge of light tonight.

Really, it's just the Tasman Bridge which connects the western and eastern shores with the River Derwent running black beneath. At night with nothing else around, the bridge becomes this beacon of light with cars twinkling all along.

It's so pretty that you wouldn't know it had such tragedy connected to it – or that maybe the most famous photo of the original bridge is one that looks like something from an action movie, with two cars teetering on the edge where road should be.

It's a three-minute trip to get from the western shore of Hobart to the eastern via the bridge, but after its collapse those three minutes became 90. Eliminate one little bridge that connects people and see the way community suffers . . . like how the crime-rate on the eastern shore increased, partly believed to be linked to slower response times of the western-shore police. It also created this huge separation between people in the east and west, not just physically and sociologically, but even psychologically – people became angrier because their morning commute was horrendous, ferry queues blew out and became hotbeds of rage and resentment.

All of this was not aided by the fact that the bridge took two slow years to repair.

Memories play like an old-school projector in my mind. I look over and it's suddenly daylight, with Lottie behind the wheel wearing her big tortoiseshell Oliver Goldsmith sunglasses. Window down, her elbow crooked and resting there while the wind whips her curled red hair into a dancing flame. 'What people really missed was the art and culture,' I can hear Lottie saying, and I must have been eleven or twelve, because Lottie's sitting taller than me and she's doing all the talking – plugging the gaps of my silence. 'The east were missing all the fun stuff. The cinemas, theatres, bookshops, galleries, museums, gardens and restaurants were all on the western shore.' We take a turn and Lottie grips the wheel with both hands, then flashes me a smile once we straighten up and she can go back to driving languidly. 'Everything that brings people together, and lets them connect with each other, whether they know it or not, is art. And if you take that away, people tend to lash out.'

The image of Lottie from my memory fades, and I'm back in the passenger seat beside Yael, with nothing but the rumble of the vintage Holden EH wagon purring gently beneath us.

The car is electric blue, with pristine white leather bench-seating and updated with a blue chrome dashboard. It's on loan from the Lovinger garage, an original of Harvey's that's been fitted with six cylinders and more stuff I really don't care about. I'd never choose to drive it because it's the size of a small boat and just as hard to manoeuvre, especially around the winding uphill streets of Battery Point and Rose Bay, where we're currently heading. But as with most things connected to Yael, she makes it all look so easy.

I lean into my corner of the car and watch her steering, looking like a *Mad Men* character with her hands on the pencil-thin wheel, humming along to 'Brass in Pocket'.

'Are you wearing a cape?' I ask her, after really getting a chance to admire her black-on-blue outfit and the intricately sparkly thing around her shoulders.

She laughs. 'No! I'm not Phantom of the Opera – it's a *capelet*!' she corrects.

'Where'd you find it?'

'It's one of Esther's, from the Rose Room cupboard.'

Esther Lovinger, nee Lovett; who appeared in Allied propaganda films of World War II, whose 'blow-me-a-kiss' was a pin-up art bestseller, second in sales only to Betty Grable's infamous 'over-the-shoulder'.

And it suddenly strikes me as odd, how casually we can talk about our long-dead ancestors and yet. 'Do you think it's weird that we don't know many dead people?'

Yael looks over at me, from all the way on the other side of the car's bench seat, and laughs. 'Repeat that back to me?'

'I'm serious. We've never really lost anyone before, but we are surrounded by artefacts of our dearly departed relatives. I mean, you're currently driving one. You don't think it's a little . . . odd?'

'Somebody's feeling morbid.'

Maybe I am. Is that okay? Is that normal?

'Hey, Ellie – do me a favour and table the tombstone talk for tonight, okay?' Before I can answer, she adds, 'You already have a reputation with these people.'

I sit up a little straighter. 'What are you talking about?' Yael's sudden silence is very concerning. 'You said this was just some random party you heard about through a friend of a friend – that's what you said.'

Yael waves her hand and then expertly steers us around a corner. 'A friend of a friend from high school.'

I ball my fists and suck in a breath as Yael's words sink in. She's talking about the same high school that I attended for a brief period of time, before I was forced to leave.

I blink and breathe, shake my head and then manage to unfurl my voice from where it plummeted deep in my stomach at Yael's revelation. 'We're going to a party in October, with people who made my life miserable and bullied me relentlessly?'

Yael sighs as she puts her blinker on. 'It's not a school thing, Ellie! And besides, it'd be people from my year level, not yours. And even if there are kids from your year, they were just being kids, and we've all graduated and are more mature than that now.' I clench my balled fists again, feeling my nails dig into palms as Yael adds, 'Anyway – this is Hobart. Six degrees of separation is more like two. You're bound to bump into someone from school just by leaving the house, so just chill. And what does October have to do with anything?!'

'Are you serious?' I practically spit the words.

She shakes her head at the road as we take yet another bend, now getting into the thick of Rose Bay suburbia.

'Halloween month, Yael.'

She huffs as we pull into a cul-de-sac where cars line either side of the street, and at the end is a house that looks more like a spaceship. It's very 1960s, all white and rounded with a flat-top roof and an entire wall of windows curved at the front, lit up and showing people already milling about inside.

As if they reserved a spot just for her, Yael sails the wagon right into the driveway, turns the key and cuts the engine – then turns bodily to look at me.

She goes to talk, and then I watch as her eyes take me in and she raises an eyebrow at my balled, white knuckles. Very carefully she reaches over to cover my fist with her hand, like she's paper and I'm rock. 'Ellie, I promise you – there's no trick here. I'm not trying to do anything to you, except get you out of that house and out of your own head a bit too.'

The light from the window is beaming down on us and lighting her up. I can see Yael's face is sincere and her brow is creased just a little bit in concern. She gently squeezes her hand over mine until I flatten my fists and she pulls away.

But even if I believe her right now, in this moment, I realise I'm not ready to tell her everything. Not about the movie and Lottie, those 'kids just being kids' who made my life hell – not any parts of it that make up a whole bigger picture. And as soon as I realise that I've got no intentions of having a deep-and-meaningful with Yael tonight, it's almost like a weight lifts and I can breathe normally again.

'Okay, I believe you,' I sigh.

'Thank you.'

The thumping of my heart eases a bit, and I dry my now-sweating palms on the knees of my jeans, wincing a little at the fading indents my nails have left.

'You'll see,' Yael adds. 'It's not going to be as bad as you think, and I bet most people won't even recognise you.'

TEN

Somebody has recognised me.

He's all the way across the room. It's a '60s throwback room, in keeping with *The Jetsons* architecture. It has a sunken floor randomly in the middle that has bench-seating all around, adorned with many patterned cushions. He's sitting on one of these olive-green seats, and he's staring at me. Intently.

Yael and I are by the wet bar, perched on stools and drinking soda water out of Tiki glassware as people she knows congregate around her, asking for updates about Sydney, med school and how she's been.

Thankfully, nobody is much interested in me. Maybe it's because I'm wearing jeans, Converse shoes and an oversized blue turtle-neck jumper. I refuse to make eye contact or smile and I didn't do anything but shake some gel through my red hair, all of which communicates my deep desire not to be here. It could also be that Yael was maybe a little bit correct; I know there are people here that I went to school with, but everyone has grown and I can't recognise anyone in particular.

Nobody asks about Lottie either. I guess this crowd aren't up on the latest Australian theatre gossip to know she's meant to be in recovery after retiring from a stage show. When asked what she's doing in town, Yael just says she's home for a weekend break and visiting her dad, which checks out for everyone, knowing as they do that her mum Constance lives in Sydney and as she's a child of divorce, it's all a matter of juggling.

I'm really not even sure if anyone knows who I am – and I am happy to exist in this context, only as Yael Felman's cousin.

Except for this guy.

This guy across the room, still staring at me.

I can see him in the mirrored splashback behind the bar, and I watch as he not-so-discreetly holds his camera-phone up, aiming it in my direction. I turn and glare at him over my shoulder. I then watch as he tries to be casual by turning his head and pretending to have a conversation with someone next to him even though there is no one sitting either side of him.

And I swear that the old-school shutter sound of the photo-taking echoes in my brain, even though he's all the way across the room. I start to hear my heart pounding; my breathing gets shallow and I can feel the redness of embarrassment like a rash, creeping up from my neck to my cheeks. And then it takes all of my energy to concentrate on the sound of my heart, my breath in and out, and the hot creep on my skin. I need to focus on them, keep myself under control and not let anyone see.

Here's where old acting habits and warm-up techniques help. I know breathing exercises. Every performer has access to them, like a box of tricks they can pull out and dust off. Different exercises for lower (diaphragmatic), middle (intercostal) and upper-chest (clavicular) breathing. My favourite from when I was a theatre kid was imagining a balloon expanding and contracting inside of my upper torso. I focus on this, on the balloon shrinking and expanding with every breath I suck in and blow out.

I don't really know how much time has passed or how many imaginary chest-balloons I've blown up before I feel Yael gently tug on my jumper sleeve, and then we're getting up and walking across the room to stand by the big front windows with a group of people. I can't grasp what they're saying because my breathing has only just evened out, my heart is finally beating normally, and checking my reflection in the windows I see that the flush has left my cheeks. I don't even check on that guy who was watching me. I'm just getting back to normal and focusing on staying this way, slowly drifting away from the group to go and stand with my back to a wall to melt into scenery.

And then a girl comes bounding up to me.

That's the only way to describe it – bounding. Practically leaping. She has this big wide smile on her face and long, curly, black hair in a half-up half-down do that perfectly frames her flushed face. She's even a little out of breath by the time she comes up to me having bounded this way.

She's wearing Mary Jane shoes, black pleated pants and a black work shirt that's a little tight on her curvy frame. She's adorned the tips of her shirt collar with something that's linked by a silver chain hanging around her neck. Not to mention she's also got on bright red suspenders – one strap of which has a silver nametag pinned on it, that I can only read once she's standing right in front of me. It reads 'Riya' and then underneath that 'State Cinema' in Art Deco font.

Up close, I can now see those tips on her collar are miniature clapper-boards. Those devices that people snap in front of cameras right before a director yells, 'Aaaaaand – action!'

'It's you!' are the first words this bounding, curly-haired creature says to me.

And because I'm a little taken aback by her, and the smile she's beaming, I can only think to say in return, 'It's me.'

'Cousin Arin finally came through, for once!'

It's then I notice the guy – the one from earlier, of the intense stare and not-so-covert photo-snapping – is standing behind this Riya. His shoulders are hunched and his hands deep in his jean pockets. He lets out an indignant, 'Hey!' after she says this.

Riya spins around to shrug at him. 'Sorry, but it's true.' She whips back around to me so fast that her curly hair smacks her in the face, not that she seems to notice. 'He once sent me a photo of his new chemistry teacher because he swore it was Jamie Lee Curtis!'

'I did not,' Arin says, looking pleadingly at me, before focusing back on Riya. 'I just said she *looked* like her! I didn't think it was *actually* Jamie Lee Curtis coming to teach at Rose Bay Secondary.'

Riya ignores him but smiles and rolls her eyes at me as if we're in on this joke together. And I can't help but think my blush is back and spreading, but this time it feels like it's emanating from my chest.

'You're freaking her out,' Arin says, and Riya's smile fades slightly.

'I am. I'm so sorry!' She holds her hands up, either like she's surrendering or else doesn't want to spook me. 'It's just that I'm a huge fan! I was already on my way when Arin sent me this photo and a message, telling me to get my butt over here – but parking is a *nightmare* on this street. And then I didn't want to get my hopes up, but I did – and now you're here and it really feels like some stars are aligning.'

I can only blink at her in reply.

'Name, cousin – name would be good,' Arin hints at her.

This time Riya comically slaps a hand to her forehead, then stretches that same hand out to me. 'Riya Vaidhyanathan.'

Vy-dee-yah-nah-thun, it rolls off her tongue.

I reach for her hand. 'Ellie Marsden.'

She laughs, and lets me go. 'Believe me, *I know!*'

It's at this point that Yael appears suddenly, sidling up to me. She's trying to catch my eye as she hooks her arm through mine so we're linked; both of us facing Riya together, with Arin standing a little behind her.

'Hi, what are we talking about?' Yael's voice sounds politely concerned.

'This is Riya Vaidhyanathan and her cousin Arin,' I say, hoping I pronounced it right, 'and we were just . . .'

I don't know how to finish, but Riya jumps in. 'I was probably about to confess that I used to write *B&J* Fanfiction when I was a kid.'

'She means three years ago,' Arin helpfully adds, and I think I see Riya's eye twitch.

Yael squeezes my arm and from the corner of my eye I can see she's plastered on a broad, plastic smile. 'Look, that's great – but Ellie's just here to chill, so maybe we don't do this tonight, yeah?'

Riya gasps. 'Oh, I'm so sorry. I didn't mean anything . . .'

'No, it's fine,' I start to say, just as Yael is saying thanks and tugging on my arm to take me away.

But then Riya's next words stop us both cold. 'I was actually going to ask how your grandmother is?'

Yael finds the will to speak before I do. 'Our grandmother?'

Riya nods. 'Ms Lovinger. Lottie – I mean. Lottie Lovinger.' She shakes her head and smiles. 'I never know what to call her.'

'You know our grandmother?' Yael's words come out carefully and slowly and I feel us both holding our breath, waiting for Riya to answer.

'I don't *know her* exactly, but I was looking forward to meeting her!' When neither Yael nor I offer any further prompt, Riya continues, 'We'd been writing to her for years, since before I even joined the FNFG, and then to get word that she finally agreed to come and speak to us, at a special screening, it was everything! But we were all so sad to hear about her retirement from *The Lion's Bride* play – and the lymph nodes surgery . . .'

'FNFG?' It's Yael who manages to cling to a question, and maybe deflect from mention of Lottie's supposed surgery.

'Fright Night for Final Girls!'

Yael and I both stare at her, Arin clears his throat and Riya smiles and explains. 'Fright Night for Final Girls – it's our horror-film club.'

I turn to Yael and she turns to me, and we seem to have a whole conversation in the blink of an eye before we both turn back to Riya and Arin.

'And Lottie agreed to go to this?' Yael asks.

Riya nods. 'She did! But of course, we all understand that she can't for a little while, not until she's recovered.'

Yael tugs gently on my arm again. 'That's correct, but I'm sure if you correspond with her agents and publicist in Sydney, they can discuss the likelihood of a new meeting at a later date.'

I'm a little impressed at how much Yael sounds like an authority on this. Am I getting a preview of her doctor voice? If so then, it's kind of cool seeing my cousin in this new light.

'Oh no, that's also why I wanted to come and see you. I can't believe our luck!' Riya says, speaking directly to me. 'See, we're normally a once-a-month film club, except in October when we go all-out for Halloween, then we meet every Sunday night!'

Yael's tugging a little more forcefully now, and I'm surprised to find that it's me who's not moving. I feel stuck to the spot, watching Riya's eyes light up.

'I know Lottie – Ms Lovinger, Lottie Lovinger, your grandmother – can't come to our final meeting in October, so I was wondering if you'd like to take her place instead, for our screening of *Blood & Jacaranda*?' Riya's hands have been gesturing wildly this whole time, and now she's opened her palms out to me, imploring.

'Me?' I ask.

But Yael cuts in saying, 'Actually, we need to get going.'

Riya's face falls and her hands drop too. 'Oh, sorry – this is a lot, and you clearly have no idea what I'm talking about . . .' She swipes furiously at a tendril of her hair that's fallen loose.

'Invite her this Sunday,' Arin pipes up from behind Riya, and I'm surprised to find he's still standing there.

'Yes!' Riya claps her hands and smiles again. 'Come this Sunday, then you can see what we're all about! And I should mention it's for everyone; all people who have lived experiences of misogyny and are encouraging of inclusive and intersectional feminist theory.' This part sounds a little like she's reading from a manifesto. She wraps up by simply saying, 'We're a totally safe space to come and hang out!'

'Thanks, but we really need to get going.' Yael has now tugged me bodily and I stumble slightly as she gets us moving, walking past Riya and Arin.

But it doesn't take long before they're following – well, Riya spinning and walking with us and I think Arin turning and sluggishly hovering behind.

We make our way through the bodies in the room. Yael even has us comically jumping down into the random sunken middle and cutting across rather than going the long way around, and then we're at the front door.

'Well, it was really nice to meet you. I hope Ms Lovinger is okay! And if you do want to come along to FNFG . . .'

'Come on, Ellie,' Yael says, pulling me through the front door.

'. . . We posted all the details to your grandmother!' Riya finishes, just as the door slams and cuts her off.

It's not until we're back in the EH wagon, Yael's arm on the bench seat as she reverses us away from the spaceship, that I finally collect my thoughts enough to wonder aloud, 'What's a "final girl" anyway?'

ELEVEN

I woke up this morning to the sense of somebody staring at me. When I rolled over, I found that it was Yael. She was lying next to me in her blue silk pyjamas, seemingly waiting for me to wake up. I don't know when she snuck in, or even if she'd stayed the whole night.

'Can you do something for me?'

'Depends,' I croaked, still groggy from sleep.

'Will you come with me when I go see her?'

Her voice wobbled a little at the end, and I could see a sheen of tears starting in her eyes, which is how we both came to be sitting in Lottie's room together on this Saturday morning, a chair on either side of our grandma as we listen to the hum of the air-mattress gently moving her body.

'It's so she doesn't get bedsores,' Corinne explains. 'The air circulates and adjusts pressure every few hours.'

Yael has tears in her eyes, and I don't really know what to do except nod her way. 'She's going to be a doctor someday,' I tell Corinne.

'Really?' Corinne asks, and Yael nods.

Then Corinne looks to Lottie and says, 'You must be so proud of her.'

And it occurs to me that only Corinne unreservedly talks of Lottie in the present, still speaking to her as if she's here, including her in conversation and asking her opinion.

'I'll leave you with your grandkids then, Lottie. Just shout if you need me.' And then Corinne's gone and it's back to the sound of the air-mattress circulating.

'This is so weird,' Yael says, and I nod.

We'd already spoken to Corinne about this waiting. Lottie isn't likely to wake up and recover, but the process of winding down can take days, weeks or even a whole month. It's just a matter of her leaving when she's ready, and we don't know when that will be.

'How can I leave her like this?'

I nod again. 'There's nothing that you can do by being here though. We're just sitting and not letting her be alone, is all. There will be plenty more relatives coming, and we'll have it covered.' I smile. 'Anyway, I hear you can't be too long gone from The University of Sydney. It's very important that you go back and study for exams or whatever, and continue crushing your first year – at The University of Sydney.'

But Yael doesn't smile back at me, and I wonder if she gets my impersonation of her dad.

'What if I don't go back?'

'What do you mean?'

Yael sniffs. 'What if I just stay here?'

'Will they let you do that? Sit your exams late, maybe by correspondence or something?'

She shakes her head. 'No, I meant . . . what if I transfer, completely.'

My eyes must boggle out of my head because she sits up straighter to defend herself. 'I was thinking about it before this, but – what if I transfer to the University of Tasmania? It's a great school, and then I could come home.'

'But your mum is in Sydney?'

'And my dad is here.'

I laugh. 'Yes, and he's practically a walking advertisement for fatherly pride that you're a student there.'

'Well maybe I just don't like the vibe,' Yael says, and rolls her eyes.

'In Sydney? A bigger city that's still too small for all of you.' I gesture with my hands at her. She's managing to look effortlessly cool with perfect coiled hair, rocking a 1970s fringe jacket from yet another ancestor's cupboard. 'What's this really about?'

She's quiet for a second, looking down at Lottie, whose chest is again rising and falling steadily, her delicate eyelids flickering from dreaming.

'You remember what you said last night? About us not knowing many dead people, but being related to a few?'

Okay. When she puts it like that the idea is a little ridiculous.

'Well, I miss that.'

'What do you mean?'

'Coming home to Hobart and Lovinger House. All these connections we have to people who are no longer with us. I love that our history is here, wrapped up in the city and all these little pieces of us.'

'Okay . . .'

'I'm just saying Sydney doesn't have that, not really.'

'And it won't if you don't stay and at least try to make it home. Put down roots and – I don't know – make it your own?'

'And where do you feel at home these days, Ellie?' Yael snaps at me, and I blink in surprise before she sighs. 'Sorry, I'm just . . .'

'Lonely,' I say for her, then shrug when she frowns at me. 'I get it. I do.'

We're quiet for a bit. I'm close to explaining to Yael what I went through after all this time – but it's strange with Lottie between us, literally. And then I miss the opportunity completely when Yael clears her throat.

'Well, maybe it'll start feeling a little more like home, and a little less lonely, if some more of my relatives come and stay,' Yael says.

'Like who?'

She rolls her eyes. 'Like you, Ellie.'

'And what would I do in Sydney?'

'Whatever you wanted to! NIDA's there. Maybe you could look into applying?'

NIDA. The National Institute of Dramatic Art. The place you go in Australia if you want a career in the performing arts.

'I lied yesterday too,' Yael adds. 'You really were as good as they said. And I know you used to enjoy it, Ellie, before everything got all twisted . . .' I hold up my hand because I really don't want to hear it, and I'm thankful when Yael pivots instead. 'We could get an apartment together!'

I scoff. 'And pay for it how, exactly? My parents are not going to fund me being in Sydney just to amuse you, and your dad will be disappointed if you're no longer on campus.'

'You'll be eighteen soon.' Yael raises her eyebrows at me. 'Some money will be coming your way – that trust fund with what you earned on the movie, plus the merchandising royalties . . .'

She means the way my name and likeness were used, not only in the production of *Blood & Jacaranda*, but also in the advertising, promotion and merchandising. And believe me, nobody thought it was going to be a movie that'd have merchandise – obscure and indie as it was. But I had an iron-clad contract thanks to Lottie's agents that covered all bases and then lo and behold, it became a hit. Aforementioned cult classic. Which means my half-girl, half-werewolf changeling form has been reprinted on t-shirts and throw-pillows; I've been turned into a Funko Pop! figurine and a Halloween costume. I am well aware of that money sitting there, and how it's accumulating. My eleven-year-old self has been forever preserved in monster form in myriad tacky and grotesque horror-fuelled ways. Believe me, I know.

I shake my head.

'Ellie, come on! You earned that money; it's yours! I know you don't like the way you got it, but you may as well use it . . .'

It's right then when Lottie wakes up.

She's suddenly breathing deeply, her eyes fluttering and she's trying to raise her hand – point at something.

'Lottie! Lottie, can you hear me? It's Yael!'

But all she can do is raise her hand again – her bony index finger pointing in front of her, and her mouth opening and closing.

'Water, do you want some water?'

But then Lottie lets out a moan, and it's clear that she's in pain.

'I'll get a nurse!'

I make for the door but Corinne's already there, and another nurse behind her.

'It's okay, ladies. She's just due for her next round of morphine.'

Yael and I move out of the way, go and stand in the corner, huddling together and watching as Corinne grasps Lottie's hand and speaks to her quietly. 'Hello, Lottie, it's Corinne. You're at Creswell Hospital. We know you need some more pain relief. We're going to take care of you, okay, honey?'

And amazingly Lottie is able to nod her head, and even sink back a little into her pillows. She looks calm again and stops trying to reach for something we can't see.

It's not until Yael's hugging me that I realise I'm crying, while she's watching the nurses working, her eyes following their every move as they help Lottie ease back into sleep.

TWELVE

Yael leaves on Sunday.

Jasper and Mum both feel a little guilty, we think, that it was us who saw Lottie in that state, so they both offer to stay with her at the hospital for a bit, and it's me and Poe who send Yael off.

Hobart airport is tiny but busy. It feels like people come and go in waves as entire planeloads congregate around the handful of shops and limited seating in the middle, and then the place empties out as soon as their plane arrives and the next round of passengers ambles in.

Poe's currently buying us overpriced sandwiches at one of the little kiosks, and I watch as an older couple in front of him in the queue keep turning around and gawking, elbowing each other and whispering.

'Ten bucks on a selfie,' Yael says.

'No way – autograph, for sure.'

We watch as the woman takes a deep breath and plucks up the courage to fully turn around and smile wide at Poe. Then her mouth is running a mile a minute and her hands gesturing wildly, by which point her partner has turned around also, and is putting a gentling hand on her shoulder.

'Wait for it.'

The woman brings her hands together, creases her brow in pleading and then Poe is smiling awkwardly and nodding. Her face smooths and she looks so happy, so charmed and delighted as she turns and says something to her partner.

'Wait . . .'

And the other woman reaches for the bumbag around her waist. She unzips it and reaches in – to retrieve her mobile phone.

'Oh, *come on*!'

Yael cackles beside me as we watch her take a photo of Poe and the other woman and then they awkwardly attempt to rearrange themselves to coordinate a selfie with all three of them. The sandwich-shop girl thankfully saves Poe from having to extend his own arm and press the button when she offers to take it for them.

'They looked way too old to be into selfies,' I say, defensively.

'That ageism is what lost you ten bucks, my darling cousin.'

'Yeah, well, IOU because I don't have any money on me.'

Yael crosses her arms and keeps chuckling, and we watch Poe shuffle to the front of the queue. Amazingly, no one else looks to be in the slightest bit interested in him, or to have even noticed the brief starstruck moment he starred in.

'You know who that woman reminded me of?' Before I can answer Yael is elbowing me gently. 'The chick from the other night.'

'Riya?'

The smirk Yael throws my way instantly alerts me to my mistake – remembering her name.

'Riya, was it?'

'Something like that.' But I can feel myself blushing.

'Well, *Riya* was totally cute in her fangirling of you.'

I don't say anything, I refuse to, and so Yael elbows me again. 'Maybe you should look up that FML thing she mentioned.'

I roll my eyes. 'FNFG?'

'Oh, have you already investigated?'

I shake my head, no.

'Well, maybe you should go along to that film club or whatever, and see what it's all about?'

'Talking to a bunch of film geeks about something I'd like to permanently bleach from my memory? No thanks.'

Yael shrugs. 'Or you go along and remember what it was that got you so excited to do that film in the first place?'

We're quiet for a bit before Yael sits forward and turns to me. 'Or maybe you go just to make up for the fact that Lottie will never be able to?'

'That's not fair.'

'But it is true.'

Our deadlock is broken when Poe comes over and hands each of us a turkey on rye sandwich. And then we sit in thoughtful silence, watching the crowds of people ebb and flow all around us. All the waiting to say goodbye feels like such a muscle memory, from all the times when I was younger, and the family would troop out here to bid farewell to Lottie.

She may have been a star, but she flew economy out of Hobart and on to Sydney or Melbourne for all her jet-setting journeys. They all started from here, especially since she got seasick and avoided the *Spirit of Tasmania* at all costs.

Lottie always wore pressed slacks or pedal pushers, with a crisp, slightly oversized men's shirt with the collar popped. Brogues or espadrilles adorned her feet depending on the weather. She was like a living Nancy Meyers character, or so the women's magazines would say.

Now sitting here in the crowded airport, I realise I'm looking for her – old habits resurfaced with memories. I'm scanning the crowd, instinctively looking for the bounce and flounce of her coifed and curled red hair. I remember the way we'd get here with minutes to spare and she'd go striding along to the gate . . . It was in these brief moments, when she walked with purpose and I'd suddenly notice people noticing her, that I felt her magnetic pull. That *thing* that made her a star, made people want to keep watching her. It was here that Lottie made sense to me in that other reality of 'make-believe'.

After I'd finally grown out of thinking that Lottie could speak to me through the TV, I realised that the *Bubbe* who'd appear in various ages, costumes and forms like some sort of strange, perpetual time-traveller wasn't the same one who'd tuck me in at night and sneak me Freddo Frogs when my parents weren't looking. I also came to understand that the only other time those two sides of Lottie clashed was here, when she was in business-mode preparing for a new role while waving goodbye to her family. She'd crouch down to kiss me and I'd get a whiff of her powdery make-up and freesia perfume and feel people watching us, curious.

I shake my head at the memories – at the comfort and peculiarity of them turning me into a time-traveller of sorts too.

Yael's plane arrives twenty minutes later, and I'm surprised at the golf ball–sized lump of sadness in my throat.

She hugs me fiercely, and over my shoulder she says, 'It was good to hang out again.'

And I know she means like we used to.

We break apart and then Yael's throwing her arms around Poe and crying into his shoulder. Kaleb may technically be her grandfather, but, like me, Poe is Yael's preferred grandparent. He has that effect on our family.

'I'll try and get home again,' Yael says.

Poe cradles her face in his hand for a moment, and Yael blinks back tears. 'We'll all take good care of her,' he says.

Then I'm leaning into him as we both wave to Yael from the terminal windows as she walks out the doors and onto the tarmac. The wind blows her hair all about, but Yael just throws a hand up high and gives a peace-out sign as she heads towards the plane.

THIRTEEN

My uncles Tobin and Seth are at Lovinger House when we get home, having taken the *Spirit* over. Mum is still at the hospital, but Jasper's returned too, and it's a rare moment when I get to see my three uncles together.

None of them look like Lottie. They all take after their fathers, and it's only me and Mum who inherited the famous fiery Lovinger locks. We do all run tall though, and it's a good thing the house has such high ceilings and exaggerated doorways because with my three uncles here, the place suddenly feels like it's gotten a lot smaller.

'You okay?'

I look up to find Poe standing in the library doorway, where I retreated an hour ago when all the back-slapping and life-updating got too much for me and I just wanted some peace and privacy.

The shelves and floorboards here are made from Australian blackwood, which would make the place look dark and gothic if not for the large French doors leading out onto the balcony, and the abundance of random tiffany lamps in every colour and pattern placed on desks, cabinets and little side-tables around the room.

'Fine and dandy,' is my reply, and Poe smiles bitterly as he walks onto the large burgundy Persian rug, and comes fully into the room.

I'm sitting on the forest-green leather chesterfield lounge, facing the cold fireplace and with a little book of poetry in my hands, Anna Akhmatova's to be exact.

'Reading Russian poetry?' Poe asks, as I move my socked feet and make room for him on one end of the three-seater. 'And Soviet-era, no less.'

Poe must know it's a reflection of the mood I'm in. Don't get me wrong, I love all my uncles but Jasper, Seth and Tobin have fathers who are lawyers and politicians respectively, and they've each followed in their footsteps. When all of them get together the conversation can be a little overwhelming. Which reminds me.

'Did they say if Shane will be coming down from Brisbane?'

Poe leans back into the leather seat and runs a hand through his hair as he shakes his head. 'He will not.'

That will make two ex-husbands who are refusing to come and see Lottie on her deathbed, since Kaleb won't even make the trip from Launceston. And I wonder how my mum will cope with the fact that she can't entirely help fulfil one of Lottie's final wishes, to have everyone come and say goodbye.

'Imagine hating someone that much.'

Poe sighs. 'I can't, thankfully.'

I absentmindedly press one of the buttons on the chesterfield upholstery. 'How did you and Lottie manage to remain friends, after everything?'

He fidgets slightly, either getting more comfortable or made *un*comfortable by the question, I can't really tell. 'Well, it helped that we were friends before we got married. And working together steadily in the years after our divorce gave us a good distraction and common goals.'

Ah yes, Poe Tuhana was famously and Oscar-award-winningly the costume-designer on the film *Seven Hills*, among a handful of others with Lottie. It's another reason it remains my favourite of her filmography; the stories I've heard of how they worked together on that movie, and the little details of Poe I can spot when watching.

'Do you think it was also missing Harvey that brought you two together and helped you remain friends?'

The elephant rarely mentioned in the room is how Poe and Lottie got together – not just that it was six months after Harvey's death, but that the three of them had been the closest of friends. At one time they were the ANZ three musketeers of Tinseltown: Lottie the up-and-coming actress with a pedigree lineage, Harvey the rebel newcomer method actor, and Poe, already an award-winning designer who worked with both of them and was even instrumental in introducing them.

Having seen *Lancelot of the Lake* more times than I care to admit, I could make a comparison between Arthur, Lancelot and Guinevere for one of the great love triangles of the ages. But as far as I know, there was nothing between Lottie and Poe while Harvey was alive – even if my mum suspects otherwise. I think Lottie truly only had eyes for Harvey. And while I've never asked before now, I've always assumed that it was his death that largely brought them together.

'Grief is very powerful, and if you let it – it can consume you. And when someone reminds you that you don't get grief without overwhelming love too . . . well, it can be a lifeline,' he says.

I don't really know what to do with that. I'm not even sure if Poe is speaking about the loss of Harvey, or currently losing Lottie. But it gets me thinking, so I shift in the seat, hearing the leather squeak a little from my movement. 'I do love her, just to be clear. I just . . . I just don't know how to forgive her,' I take a deep breath, 'or what to do with all this anger I still have.'

Since I've been home, I have had this feeling that my anger is like walking on soft sand. I'm getting slowed down and sinking into it when all of a sudden, the tide comes in . . . The anger I still feel towards Lottie is sometimes rolled away by this grief, but the tide eventually goes out again and I'm back on the beach.

Poe nods once, but we both know he doesn't have an answer for me, so he stands up, sticks his hands in his pockets and leaves me to it. But before he exits the library he spins around and recites: '*You will hear thunder and remember me, and think: she wanted storms*,' and then he's gone.

It's my favourite Akhmatova line from my favourite of her poems. Of course, Poe knows it; it's his old copy I plucked from the Lovinger collection, after all, and he underlined those same exact words, once.

The thought of wanting storms – inviting chaos, maybe? – makes me think on Yael's words from earlier. Her idea that I should attend that film club, Fright Night for Final Girls. Which also makes me think of Riya.

She said they meet every Sunday night in October. I glance at the old-style gold clock with glass dome that sits on the serving table behind the couch and see that it's 5 p.m., which means theoretically, there's still time to attend.

But I don't know anything else about this club, except maybe where it takes place, flashing back to Riya's nametag. A quick Google search on my phone brings up the State Cinema website, and a mysterious link for the film club that encourages enquiring at the ticket counter, emailing, or calling and asking for Riya. I don't quite have the nerve to do any of the above, but then I remember her saying that she posted details to Lottie already . . .

I jump up from the couch, letting Anna's book of poetry fall gently to the rug, as I dash down to the blue room and straight to the clamshell dressing table, where Lottie's little stack of fan mail is still sitting.

It's a long shot, but I start rifling.

There are envelopes with postage stamps from all over– Massachusetts, Edinburgh, Taipei – and ones from Australia: Churchlands, Barton, and Phillip Island. And then I find it – a plain white A4 envelope, with a rubber stamping in the corner with the same Art Deco logo from Riya's nametag for the State Cinema on Elizabeth Street in North Hobart.

I pause before tearing it open – take a deep breath, and then rip – to find a black and white photocopied flyer full of hand-drawn illustrations and lettering – Fright Night for Final Girls. Every inch of the white paper is covered in something but right in the middle is a roughly illustrated depiction of Riya and another girl, both of them posing like Edvard Munch's *The Scream* while all around them are tiny illustrations of horror-filled things: bats, spiders, zombie-heads, hockey masks, a waning moon, scythes, coffins and cauldrons.

In small font at the top of the page are hand-drawn social-media icons made to look like they're melting. And a message that I guess explains their lack of virtual presence:

Find us, don't follow us.
We are an accessible, safe and welcoming
environment for fellow horror-film buffs.
Come and live deliciously.

And then at the very bottom of the page also in hand-lettering:

October 2019 schedule – State Cinema, North Hobart – 8 p.m. starts

Sunday 6th – *The Slumber Party Massacre*
Sunday 13th – *Tigers Are Not Afraid*
Sunday 20th – *It Follows*
Sunday 27th – *The Lure*
Thursday 31st (Halloween!) – **Blood & Jacaranda*

*** Tickets: $15 for a special one-off and exclusive guest appearance Q&A with the actor Lottie Lovinger**

FOURTEEN

The State Cinema is 106 years old.

It's an Art Deco style white building with a geometric roof of clean lines with an arch window in the middle. It is deceptively larger inside than it would appear on the outside. Only a few years ago, the new owner excavated the original site and renovated the basement levels to put in more cinemas, plus a three-storey glass tower for rooftop screenings. Out the back of the long building is also a bar and dining area, and apparently, it's become quite the tradition to bring in a glass of wine during viewings.

I haven't personally been to the cinema since it was redone. I'm more familiar with its history – *naturally* – given it tended to run alongside my family's.

The evidence of which is right in front of me – in a canvas print colour photograph hanging near the box office. It's of a much-younger Lottie with her hair down in a wild tangle, wearing a distinctive Marimekko rebel flower shift dress, and standing next to her is her *The Hazards* co-star Ryan Longford in a double-denim get-up with his over-long fringe side-swept. They're standing side-by-side and right outside the State Cinema entrance I just came through. Both their heads are turned as they watch a tall and imposing figure in a dark suit with a shock of white hair approach them; it's Prime Minister Gough Whitlam.

The next moment in this sequence of events – of Gough Whitlam and Lottie shaking hands – hangs in a hallway of Lovinger House in an antique gilt frame. On a rainy day in our childhood, Yael and I were inside bouncing a badminton shuttlecock back and forth, when I swung my racquet wildly and swatted the frame so it shuddered on the wall – and only Lottie happening to come along and place her hands either side prevented its fall.

'You two should show some respect,' she'd said, straightening the photo and then looking over her shoulder at us. 'That's Gough Whitlam – Patron Saint of Prime Ministers who Gave a Damn about the Arts,' and then she winked.

Yael and I had giggled into our hands, for the unusual combination of saints and solemnity that came from our *bubbe*. And then a story had followed – recited as Lottie took my badminton racquet and started bouncing the shuttlecock on its head as she stepped lightly up and down the hallway.

'Gough Whitlam once saw fit to save a little cinema in North Hobart when it was going under. Instead of letting it be sold off privately, Whitlam had his government buy the State Cinema, and keep it public so everyone could go on enjoying it.' Here she'd snatched the shuttlecock out of the air, then used my racquet to point back at the picture on the wall. 'I was even there on the day that Gough and Margaret Whitlam visited the newly opened AFI State Cinema in 1975 for a special screening of *The Hazards*.'

Lottie walked back to the photo on the wall and tapped her finger twice over the larger-than-life figure of Gough Whitlam. 'This was the first Australian politician who really respected the arts and artists.'

And then in a pretty convincing baritone imitation of Gough himself, Lottie quoted the ex-PM when she said, 'Don't forget girls, in Gough's own words, "A society in which the arts flourish is a society in which every human value can flourish."'

I'm standing here, in my faded jeans and vintage herringbone blazer, with a Lazertits band t-shirt underneath, looking at yet another momentous event in my family's long film history, when Riya finds me.

There's no bounding this time, but rather sidling. I feel her sidle up and stand beside me, and for just a moment we're both quiet as we admire the photo of the opening. But eventually I feel her as if she's buzzing, and she breaks the quiet.

'You're here.'

Then we both turn to each other and she's smiling at me. Her curly hair is up in a loose bun this time, with baby hairs and tendrils escaping. She's still got the red suspenders and same uniform as the other night, except this time her collar-tips are eerily life-like blue eyeballs that seem to be staring at me.

'I'm here.'

'I thought I was maybe a bit much the other night? That I'd scared you off.'

'You were very *enthusiastic*,' I say, and smile at the memory.

She laughs and tucks a loose curl behind her ear. 'That's a kinder way to put it.'

The cinema foyer and box office are plushily carpeted and also decked out in Art Deco, with soft lighting and big front windows looking out onto a quiet Elizabeth Street. Maybe it's noticing the abundance of couples that are milling about, but I realise the dreamy throwback feel of the place is rather romantic – and I suddenly feel myself blushing to be standing here facing Riya, and I work hard to compress the smile on my face into something less obvious.

But maybe I try a little too hard to come across cool and calm, because then I suddenly blurt out, 'I'm not doing the guest-appearance thing for *Blood & Jacaranda*, just so you know!'

Her smile flickers and falls. 'Oh?'

'Yeah. It's really not my place, to talk about that movie. I just thought I'd come for a one-off.'

'But – you were *in* the film?'

I feel my blush growing redder. 'It's still not something I'm interested in talking about,' I say. But then I feel bad, so I add, 'If that's okay?'

She nods and smiles again. 'Of course – but you never know, maybe we'll tempt you to participate for the Halloween event?'

'I doubt it.'

'Okay, well – in the meantime you're right on time, come and meet the club!'

Riya turns on her heel and heads down a set of stairs to the side of the foyer to what must be the new basement cinema rooms. I follow behind her, admiring the posters of Australian movies that hang on the high brick wall as we descend: *Strictly Ballroom*, *Holding the Man, The Sapphires*, *Muriel's Wedding* and *Looking for Alibrandi.*

Down here is like a little rabbit warren or wine cellar – also because there are indeed stacks of wine racks right outside the room Riya's heading towards, down one of the hallways.

I follow after her into a low-ceilinged room that's more like a family lounge, with five rows of double-seat leather couches on one side, and an entire wall of wine racks along the opposite wall. The floor is slightly slanted downwards and made of large sandstone bricks, with red rugs underneath each of the couches.

The screen down the front is projecting a single image – the same one from the photocopied flier: the club's name Fright Night for Final Girls in oozing lettering and an illustration of Riya and another girl in *The Scream* pose. And then it's like I'm seeing double when the illustrated girl appears before me and stands beside Riya.

She's not dressed in uniform like Riya is, so I assume she doesn't work here. Instead she's wearing black stockings under denim shorts, Doc Martens black boots and an oversized black hoodie jumper with FIGHT EVIL, READ BOOKS printed in large white font on the front. Her hair is short and blonde, but unlike mine hers is definitely in a stylish pixie cut. And she has a pretty, pointed face and brown eyes that look a little wide as they take me in.

Riya stands between us and says, 'Ms Marsden, this is my best friend and co-president, Jen Jones – Jen, this is . . .'

'Ellie is fine,' I say.

Riya very deliberately points at me and says, 'Ellie,' then continues moving her hands – something she's been doing the whole time she's been talking. When she said my name, she also tapped her right pointer finger to her left hand, for what I realise must be each letter of my name.

Because Jen is Deaf.

This is confirmed when Riya's hands stop moving and Jen's take over. She gives me a small wave, and then her hands start flying, ending in one going to her chin flatly and moving back to me.

'Jen says hello, she can't believe it's you and *thank you* for being here. She also – *we* also – hope that your grandmother is feeling better?' Riya says.

'Oh – um – you're welcome?' I've turned to Riya as I say this. I watch her translate it to Jen. When Riya stops moving, I say, 'And thank you.'

'I think you meant to say that to Jen and not me,' Riya says, gently.

I realise she's not who I'm speaking to – so I say it again, facing Jen, while Riya's hands move for me. 'And thank you, yes, Lottie's . . . on the mend.'

I dread saying more, when a trio of voices come from the door to save me, and I spin around to find three girls suddenly stop moving and talking to just stare at me, their jaws practically on the floor.

'Little Mate,' one of them manages to squeak while looking right at me.

She's short and looks younger than me, Jen and Riya – maybe about 13? The other two look a little taller and older, but not by much.

'Ellie, this is Kate, Maria and Ah-Pei.' Each girl gives a hesitant little finger-wave as Riya says their names. The youngest who called me by my character's name was the last – Ah-Pei – and she definitely looks the most overwhelmed.

'Riya – um – what the hell?' one of the taller girls, Maria, says 'Explain!' She pushes the other two more fully into the room to come and stand in front of me.

I don't turn around, but I can feel rapid movement before Riya speaks again, as Jen. 'Everyone chill out. Ellie Marsden is here as our guest, and just to see what we're all about. Let's treat her as a human being and not . . .'

But before she can finish, Ah-Pei blurts out, 'You gave me nightmares when I was a kid!'

'You're still a kid,' Kate laughs.

'No, now I'm 14 and they're self-inflicted nightmares because I'm addicted to scares,' Ah-Pei shoots back. And after she says this, she's smiling at me and her eyes have become a little glazed as she continues to stare.

It's Jen who brushes past me to come and stand in front of Ah-Pei. Jen makes a peace sign with both her hands and then rolls her wrists to the right.

'Relax.'

Riya is standing beside me and practically whispering the translation right into my ear. She's so close I can smell her scent of something citrus, and I have to control myself not to take a deep breath in that instant.

Jen, Ah-Pei, Kate and Maria share more rapid hand movements that Riya doesn't translate, which must mean it's not for me to know. Instead she takes a step back and gestures to one of the couches in the second row, inviting me to sit down, which I do, while she goes to the front of the room.

Once I'm seated, the other girls settle on the couches behind me, and then Jen goes to close the door.

'Oh, aren't there more people coming?' I ask, even though I'm not sure how many more could fit into this smaller cinema room. I swear I think I see Riya's eye twitch.

Her hands move, telling Jen what I just asked, as she makes her way to the front of the room. I think I can also see them share a secret conversation using just their eyebrows.

'This is the film club, officially,' Riya says.

'Five members?'

'We're very exclusive.'

I laugh because I feel like I'm missing something obvious. And maybe I should point out that their cagey Internet presence can't help with membership. But then Riya pulls focus again and I remain silent.

'Shall we begin?' Riya claps her hands once and then uses them to say 'I wish to acknowledge with deep respect that when we meet here, we do so on the lands of the Paredarerme people – the true and Traditional Owners of this area of nipaluna, or Hobart, that runs along the Derwent River. I would also like to pay my respects to their Elders; past, present, and emerging; and to reassert the knowledge that Aboriginal sovereignty was never ceded.'

And then it's Jen who takes over, her hands moving quickly. Riya translates for my benefit. '*The Slumber Party Massacre* is a 1982 American slasher film written by feminist Rita Mae Brown and intended as a satirical parody of the genre. It was directed by Amy Holden Jones, who made it into straight horror.'

During Jen's speech, I can only guess that the sign for *party* must be the pinkie fingers twirling, and when Jen holds her arms up as if firing a rifle, it's also clear that that must be the sign for *massacre.*

Jen continues. 'It's exactly as it promises – a massacre at a slumber party and a killer on the loose, his weapon of choice is a power drill and see if you can't spot the phallic symbolism throughout.'

Ah-Pei, Kate and Maria whoop behind me, as Jen makes a certain sign – tapping one of her fingers to the tip of her nose – and I can't help but laugh.

'Amy Holden Jones was 27 when she directed the film, having been tutored by a big name in schlock horror – Roger Corman – since she was 22,' Riya says and signs. 'You can definitely see the questionable influence of Corman, and probably the studio too, in much of the gratuitous boob and butt shots throughout.'

The girls boo, loudly, behind me.

'But it's worthy of viewing and discussion for the sexual agency the girls express, the fact that no boyfriends come to the rescue and it's entirely up to the girls to save themselves with determination and brains.' Riya smiles and rolls her eyes. 'Plus you'll have to admit, the symbolic breaking of the drill-bit is very funny.'

Jen wraps things up. 'Roger Corman would go on to produce two loose sequels in *Slumber Party Massacre II* and *III*, all of which had female directors – making this the first and only horror franchise directed entirely by women.'

'So without further ado, we give you – *The Slumber Party Massacre*!' With that, Riya dashes down the aisle and to the back of the room and then the lights go out and the movie screen with the photo of her and Jen goes blank before the feature begins to play.

And I'm surprised when Riya comes back and sits beside me. Landing on the other side of my couch with a soft thud, she pulls out a packet of Maltesers from I don't know where and offers me one.

Jen takes the couch in front of us, and from where I'm seated, I can see she has something like a large beeper – those things from the 80s before people had mobile phones. I watch it light up with scrolling text I can't quite make out.

'It's a TitleCap,' Riya explains, when she sees me looking. 'It makes older movies like this – made before subtitles were widespread – accessible for her. Scrolling text on the TitleCap relays sound action and dialogue, but it's kind of clunky having to look down at the device for subtitles, and up at the screen for action. Jen calls them Title*Craps*.'

'Oh, it seems like there should be more advanced technology than that?'

Riya rolls her eyes and nods her head. 'Tell us about it! We're looking to get some funding for updated devices, especially because this is the last functioning TitleCap the cinema has. All the others are broken beyond repair.'

And then the three girls behind shush us and Riya giggles, leans into me and whispers, 'Are you ready for this?' just as the film starts with keyboard-horror titles and a boy on his bike doing a paper round.

'Probably not,' I whisper back, as the camera pans up to a California bungalow and through a top-storey window. Then for literally no reason at all, it shows a girl naked – except for her underpants – getting ready for school.

FIFTEEN

Riya is standing with me off to the side and in a little alcove in the main cinema foyer. 'There's something about this place that's missing, but I can't put my finger on it?' I muse out loud,

'Popcorn.'

I turn to her. 'What?'

'There's no popcorn. The owner says it cheapens a place and ruins the theatre-going experience, so . . .'

'That's it! There's no popcorn smell!'

'And I am thankful every day,' Riya says, nodding and smiling as she punctuates this declaration.

Then we're back to silence and standing awkwardly.

'So – did you like the film?'

My face must give everything away because Riya laughs. 'Oh no, I'm never going to see you again, am I?' she says.

For some reason, her saying this carves out a little hollow in my chest – and the only thing stopping me reaching my hand up to place it over the spot that feels slightly indented now is noticing that when she smiles, only one of her cheeks get a little dimple, right in the middle.

'You ready for ice cream?' Maria has walked up to us, her arm linked through Ah-Pei's, who is still looking up at me a little strangely. 'We always do ice cream and chats after a movie, in the café out back,' Maria further explains.

I shake my head. 'No, I should be getting home – thank you, though.'

It's my turn for a morning with Lottie tomorrow.

'Can I get a selfie?' Ah-Pei blurts out, and I feel both Maria and Riya wince in response.

I don't know how to politely decline as my heart starts racing, but then Riya does it for me. 'Let's just live in the moment, okay? Maybe you can get a photo another day,' she says.

Ah-Pei's face falls but she doesn't say anything else, and I mouth 'thank you' to Riya when Ah-Pei walks away.

'Well, I better head off,' I say, and Riya asks where I'm parked and offers to walk me.

'Well, that could take a while – since I walked here myself.'

Her eyes widen. 'From where?'

'Battery Point.'

'Why? It's a ten-minute drive! Walking must have taken you – what? Forty minutes?'

'Well, I'd need to borrow one of my family's cars and they're all vintage, wide and boat-like, so I'm avoiding driving at the moment.'

Riya nods once, then calls across the emptying foyer to the others. When everyone turns so does Jen, and Riya speaks while signing and walking towards them. 'Hey, I'm going to drive Ellie home – so I'll let Jen take the lead on the discussion, okay?'

'Oh, you don't have to do that!' I say, but Riya waves me away.

I'm a little surprised that she didn't even ask if I intended to use a taxi or ride-share app, which I did. But I find myself not wanting to plant the idea in her head, so I remain silent and watch as she hugs each of the girls in turn. Then she comes back to me and holds up a finger to say one minute. She ducks behind the box office and into a door there that reads 'Staff Only'.

She emerges a moment later with a purple messenger bag slung across her shoulder and a bright purple raincoat on.

'Ready?' she asks, and then I'm following her to the back of the building, down more hallways and out a back door that leads to a small staff carpark.

I follow a purple-clad Riya like she's a beacon to one of the last cars in the lot.

'I hope you don't have a general aversion to vintage,' she says, as she approaches a red car, and then opens her arms out wide in a *TA-DA* motion, 'because this is a classic 2001 Volkswagen Jetta!'

'Wow.'

'Please, contain your excitement.'

'No, it's . . . really . . .'

'What I could afford,' Riya says. She unlocks the door and motions for me to get in. Somehow it almost feels colder inside the car than out.

Riya sticks the key in and turns it, and then straight away she reaches over to crank up the heat. 'Give it a second to kick in,' she says. She leans back in her driver's seat, so I do the same in the passenger.

There's an easy silence as we listen to the whir of the heating, but there's something that's been niggling at me all evening, so I clear my throat. 'So it's a little hard to get intel, because I couldn't find a website or socials for you, but you said FNFG is a feminist film club, right?'

Riya whips her head to the side and stares at me. 'You tried searching for me?' I think I see her blush, but can't really tell in the dim carpark light. 'I mean *us* – you tried searching for us?'

I nod once and she winces slightly. 'Yeah, I guess being fans of horror has made us paranoid, and we don't *really* trust the big tech of social media . . .'

I can appreciate that. The two accounts I used to have were always set to private, I was militant about not being tagged in anything by my friends, and then only a few months ago I wiped them completely and haven't glanced at them since. All fuelled by my worst paranoid nightmares of winding up on another gossip site, or TMZ listicle of 'How These Child Actors Look Now!'. Shudder.

Riya sighs. 'We're also an intersectional feminist horror film club and when we did briefly have social media accounts, we spent more time blocking and reporting trolls – which has also put me off having personal accounts for a little while, especially during Year 12, when I do not need the distraction.' At this, Riya shudders slightly too, but it could just be from chill.

I take a deep breath and say the other part to this that I've been quietly musing on: 'Isn't it kind of an oxymoron for a horror-film club to be feminist? I mean, the genre is all about violence, blood and gore, monsters and serial killers – a little hard to find celebrations of feminism in all that, right? And if the movie tonight was meant to be the best example of what's on offer . . .'

Riya shakes her head, adamantly. 'Hey, don't hate on *Slumber Party Massacre*! It earned its place in the pantheon . . .' She sighs.

'But yeah, okay – I wish you'd been here in July when we did Julia Ducournau's *Raw*, or in August when it was Ana Lily Amirpour's *A Girl Walks Home Alone at Night*!'

When all I can do is shrug, Riya lets out a groan and comically raises her fists to the roof of her Jetta. When she brings them down, she looks at me again. 'And you're wrong, by the way.' When I raise my eyebrows and motion with my hand for her to continue, she does. 'Just because the horror genre is scary, bloody or violent doesn't make it inherently anti-women or automatically anti-feminist; that's just as bad as the assumption that women should only associate with *nice*, *clean*, *pretty*, *feminine* things – like rom-coms and Jane Austen adaptations.' Riya manages to both flutter and roll her eyes as she emphasises this list, and I kick up a smile.

She goes on. 'Horror is one of the few genres that ever puts women's fears under the microscope and encourages audiences to cheer them on as they conquer them in leading roles.' Riya takes a deep breath before she says, 'And none of this is surprising, considering that modern horror was – in many ways – invented by a teenage girl.'

I let out a sarcastic laugh. 'Excuse me?'

At this, Riya practically bounces in her seat to tell me. 'Hello? – Mary Shelley!'

When all I can do is shrug again, Riya looks exaggeratedly shocked. 'Tell me you know who Mary Shelley is!'

I roll my eyes. 'Yeah, yeah – *Frankenstein*.'

'No "yeah-yeah" about it; Mary was 19 years old, had eloped with a married man, was disowned by her family, on the run from creditors, and winds up at this secluded house party on

Lake Geneva where – as well as being stuck with blowhard Lord Byron – it's been raining for eight weeks straight thanks to a volcanic eruption the previous year that throws the whole world's weather patterns out of whack.'

I turn in my seat more fully as Riya gets stuck into the story, hurriedly pushing wisps of hair out of her face and gesturing wildly with her hands as she speaks.

'So Lord Byron, bored one night, lays down this challenge to see who can write the scariest ghost story. He's *totally* wanting an opportunity to remind Mary that she's inferior in all ways, but especially creatively, to all the men in the room – her poet husband among them. But what does Mary do?'

I shake my head.

'Our girl Mary ends up totally upending the rules of literature and shocking modern society by writing the first non-religious creationist myth in *Frankenstein: The Modern Prometheus* – throwing in a healthy dose of side-eye about the hubris of man – all while effectively inventing the modern science-fiction and horror genres as we know them.'

'I haven't read it, but is *Frankenstein* technically not a ghost story?'

Riya rolls her eyes. 'So she lost the bet with Byron but won on infamy. The fact still remains: horror was invented by a disenfranchised teenage girl, and there are plenty of brilliant examples of feminism in the genre throughout the ages – *Slumber Party Massacre* included.'

With that, Riya finally turns the car over and starts the engine, also letting a song come through on what I think is an old-school CD player. She backs us out of the parking lot and adds, 'Besides, if horror was really against everything feminism stands for, FNFG wouldn't exist in the first place.'

'Yeah, about that too – what's a final girl anyway?'

Riya smiles as she grips the wheel to execute a tight turn and get us on the road. 'Ah, the final girl is a familiar trope in horror. She is the sole survivor, the one left standing at the end of a film. She alone will confront the monster or killer at the end of the movie and live to tell the tale – or else appear in the sequels to create a film franchise.' Riya glances at me and then back to the road. 'Sigourney Weaver as Ellen Ripley in the *Alien* franchise, Neve Campbell as Sidney Prescott in the *Scream* films . . .' she takes a breath before adding, 'Your grandmother actually helped create the archetype, FYI, in *The Hazards*. She went a long way to defining the role of female survival in the genre, thanks to those films.'

I shift to slide my hands beneath my denim-clad thighs, both to warm them and so I can dig my nails into the seat. 'I've never seen them,' I say.

We just so happen to pull up to a red light, so Riya can punctuate her 'What?!' with a slightly forceful and well-timed brake.

I shrug. 'Well, technically I've been unable to see any of them due to rating restriction, but also – horror just isn't my thing.' I've pitched for nonchalance with my reply. I'm channelling a degree of carefree that I just don't feel, not really, but projecting and feeling are almost the same thing and it's all about acting to get the balance right.

I wait to see if Riya intends to mention the obvious – my status as one of the definitive monsters of my age – but she doesn't. Instead once the light turns green and we're moving again, I further deflect by asking another burning question. 'Speaking of, how is it that Ah-Pei is able to watch these movies when she's only 14?'

Riya chuckles. 'Her parents signed a permission slip, basically – all of our guardians did. But Ah-Pei in particular, it's because her dad is very supportive of her obsessions, partly because he's the Arts and Culture editor for the *Hobart Town Gazette*, so they're very egalitarian.'

I laugh and look out the window at the streetlamps and house lights of Battery Point, scattered among an otherwise dark blue world at night. The music coming through Riya's radio is a woman's deep, soulful voice singing about trying to settle down to write, while a piano riffs along.

'What's this music?'

'You like it? It's Radha Thomas – this awesome Indian jazz singer I've been obsessed with for years.' Riya glances over at me quickly and then adds, 'She went a long way to me figuring out I was gay, because I had such a crush on her voice and, like, the *idea* of her as I listened to all those early albums . . .'

When Riya looks back at me to see how I've taken this confirmation, I smile gently and watch as she takes a deep breath and her shoulders ease a little. Her arms are no longer so rigidly stretched in front of her on the steering wheel.

I look away and smile to myself privately too at how that little anecdote was as smooth as the sultry jazz we're listening to at getting a small but important point across.

And before I can muse any longer on how something has eased within my chest, we're climbing and winding around the streets of my suburb until we get to the wrought-iron gates of Lovinger

House. Riya pulls her car just onto the lip of our driveway and turns the engine off. It occurs to me that I didn't have to navigate our way here – she just knew exactly where to go.

Just then, Riya lets out a low whistle. 'I can't believe you actually live here.'

'Lived,' I correct her. 'I'm just staying for . . .' I don't quite know how to finish this sentence, since I can't go into my real reason for returning, and I don't think I'll be going back to boarding anytime soon. So instead I quickly say, 'I'm just home for a little while.'

Thankfully, Riya is still too preoccupied with gazing out the windshield to notice my evasive answer. She shakes her head, and then looks to me, smiling but also seeming a little embarrassed. 'Not to be weird, but I've always wondered what it's like inside.'

'Old, mostly – and pretty cluttered,' I shrug, 'and I guess my family have convinced themselves that it's not hoarding if its heirlooms.'

When Riya laughs, it's on the tip of my tongue to say that maybe she'd like to come over some day for a tour. But as Riya's laughter dies out into a breathy chuckle, I let the silence go on too long and then we're both sitting there, a little awkwardly until she clears her throat.

'So, anyway – you should definitely get your hands on a copy of *Frankenstein*. I mean, since we probably can't be friends until you've read it,' she says.

I don't know what to say. The cold is rushing in now that the car is off. My blazer is too thin against the Hobart-evening chills and my brain feels like it's frozen slightly too on Riya's 'friends' and whether or not there was emphasis on the word.

'Oh, well – to avoid that tragedy I will one day get around to it,' I quickly say, realising my silence has gone on too long.

Riya nods. 'Also – if you wanted to – I could give you a few tutorials on horror movies . . . feminist, specifically. Only if you were keen?'

My heart jolts at this, and my brain unfreezes – only to go into a complete spin-cycle of not knowing what to do. It's like trying to read between the lines of a play to find the subtext of everything the character wants to say but is withholding. My dad says that's where an actor's power lies: between the lines and performance and melding the two into something richer, deeper and true.

But while I've been trying to figure out my own lines and the possible meanings behind hers, the silence has been stretching between us and I've missed my cue completely.

'Or not!' Riya says hastily. 'Totally okay, but – you know where to find me. I'm six days a week at the cinema, saving up for uni and paying off this car . . .'

'It's a great car!' I blurt out, trying to make up for my quiet.

Riya laughs again. 'Thursday is my day off, just so you know.'

And then I'm looking at her and she's looking at me. There's the glow from a streetlamp casting us in an orange haze, and I have this sudden urge to reach over and tuck a loose curl behind her ear.

But I don't. My beats are off, the rhythm lost. I still feel like I'm just out of step and missing my mark . . . so instead I nod once and reach for the door handle, pull on it three times. Riya tells me to jiggle it a little, and then the door pops open and I'm taking a big gulp of cold Hobart air and turning around and bending down to thank her for the ride home.

She waits as I slip between the wrought-iron gates and start trekking my way up the driveway, hugging my elbows against the cold. I don't think she can see me anymore, but then I hear a sudden *HONK!* so I spin around.

The streetlamp light is still casting down on her, so I can just make out that she's rubbing her forehead with one hand, while muttering to herself. I can see her mouth moving, but I can't even begin to guess what she's saying, which makes me smile. I watch as she backs out of my driveway, and then vanishes into the night.

The whole rest of the way up the drive I'm wondering if I should've given her my number, or else asked for hers. Then I doubt if it's even okay to feel this way – with everything that's happening?

There's no one around to see me pondering all of this; only the old gothic house waiting for me at the top of the hill. A few windows lit up within, and a backdrop of starry Hobart skies strung up like a banner to welcome me home.

SIXTEEN

I find my mum in the front sitting room again on Monday morning, taking her tea and reading the paper on the long sofa.

'Where'd you sneak off to last night?' she says, before I've even entered the room.

The question catches me by surprise, and then my foot catches against the leg of an occasional table with an antique vase sitting on it, one that I am vaguely aware belonged to a great-aunt who acted in radio plays during the war. I reach out to right the vase, and then I right myself, but I glare at the dainty walnut table anyway.

The trip also gives me a moment to compose myself and decide to deflect Mum's question. I'm not sure how to tell her about Riya and the film club, it somehow feels – inappropriate? With all we're going through.

'This place is like a museum – filled with a bunch of dead people's junk,' I hastily observe. And then I wince at the poor choice of deflection. Doubly so when Mum's head rises above the *Hobart Town Gazette* she's reading, and her eyes go to the mantelpiece on the opposite side of the room, a British Academy Film Award sitting there. And I wince knowing it's Harvey's.

Over a few centuries, my family have acquired something like eighteen AACTAs, four Emmys, five BAFTAs, three Golden Globes, six gold Logies, a couple of Oscars and countless various others. We don't have a trophy room. That's far too gauche and, honestly, most awards are awkward, heavy things and the collective weight of them in one room would probably sink the foundations. We've donated a lot to museums and private charitable organisations, sold a few to collectors, and maybe one or two were also sold to Hard Rock Cafés. But we've got Adam Lovinger's Oscar on display, and Harvey Hutton's handful of silverware too. They don't particularly have pride of place anywhere, just on any given mantel – and Harvey's happens to be here.

'I'm sorry,' I stammer, and come to stand in front of my mum.

She lowers the paper into her lap and reaches for her cup of tea, waving me away as she has a sip.

I take a seat beside her, curling one of my legs underneath myself so I can face her and the mantel. 'I never really asked you before, what it was like growing up here – around all this *stuff*.'

She raises an eyebrow at me. 'You grew up here too, may I remind you?'

'Yeah, but I didn't know any of the dead relatives, not personally. But he was *your* dad.'

Mum places her mug back onto the dainty side-table, then turns to me more fully. 'He was, but the truth is – I didn't really know him. It's funny; sometimes memories will come to me so clearly, like scenes in a movie, and I'll realise, *oh – that's why*!'

She shakes her head. 'I more remember having this feeling that my dad was never really happy, or himself.'

She gets a kind of faraway look, so to pull her back I say, 'Poe was talking to me about Harvey, just yesterday.'

Another look passes over my mum's face – this time it's like a cloud obscuring the sun, a strange shadow passing and then gone. 'You better get going, Ellie. It's nearly time for you to be at the hospital.'

And then she gathers her paper and mug, rises from the couch and walks out.

•

Back at Lottie's bedside, the room has started to feel empty even with us in it. For the first time since I started sitting vigil, I feel the need to fill the space up with the sound of my voice.

'It turns out, you're a final girl,' I say, to throw some sound around. 'The one to survive to the end of a movie – last one left standing.'

Only Lottie's machines beep at me in reply.

'Yeah, I know – ironic. But apparently it's kind of a big deal in horror films.'

More beeping.

'I guess maybe I should go to the Lovinger library and hunt down those DVDs of *The Hazards*, huh? See what Riya was talking about . . .' I shake myself. 'Riya is this girl. I think you maybe know her – knew her? She co-runs a horror film club, out of the State Cinema? And speaking of, that photo of you and Gough is hanging up there too, like the one in our hallway you told me and Yael about?' I clear my throat, and in an imitation of

Lottie's imitation of Whitlam's baritone, I begin to say, '"A society in which the Arts flourish –"'

I snap my mouth shut as two nurses pause outside Lottie's room to have a brief chat about a patient. I shift in my seat and wait a moment even after they've moved away, before speaking again.

'Anyway – you agreed to attend this film club. In case you didn't know – maybe your agents even arranged it for you? I'm not sure. I really can't picture you going along and talking to these girls . . . then again, I couldn't picture me going along and talking with them either. But I did – last night, kind of. Yael told me to, and I guess I'm still eight years old and I do everything that she tells me to.'

Lottie has started receiving flowers. Only a few, but now her room has carnations, roses and even a bunch of daffodils. They're evidence that my mum is slowly getting the word out about her condition. Some of the cards attached are the who's who of Hollywood from a certain era. The room is starting to smell like the gardens of St David's Park too, and I wonder if my mum and uncles also felt that the room needed livening up.

'I didn't stay and chat with them – the film club, I mean. I watched a truly terrible movie and left. But then I kind of spoke to Riya, because she gave me a ride home.' I smile. 'You'd have called her "chivalrous". She's offered to explain horror movies to me, and I think she was maybe also offering to go on a date? I really don't know. I think it'd be weird because she's clearly a fan of yours, and I think mine too? That's got to be crossing some sort of ethical line, right?'

Just then, Corinne bustles into the room, armed with the lotion she uses to keep Lottie's hands from cracking.

'Morning, Ellie!'

She pulls a chair up to the other side of her bed and reaches for Lottie's hand. 'Good morning Ms Lovinger, and how are we today? It's Corinne, sweetie.'

I watch as she slowly starts working the cream into Lottie's hands, ever so gently, and then she glances up at the TV in the corner of the room and rolls her eyes.

'Ugh, I hate this movie,' she says.

It's *Gone with the Wind* and I'm a little thrilled at Corinne's response, because it truly is an awful film.

'Lottie hates it too,' I say, before correcting. '*Hated*, I mean.'

Corinne glances at me and smiles. 'Right on, Lottie! Don't even get me started on how Hattie McDaniel was mistreated . . . And I can't believe anyone ever praises it as an epic romance. I personally think *The Hazards* was more romantic!'

'I was just talking about that movie with her.'

'Oh yeah?'

I nod. 'Yeah, I've been trying to do what you do and actually, you know, talk to her like she's here.'

Corinne opens her mouth then closes it, and then I see something pass over her face and she seems to think better of it.

'She is here,' she says gently.

I feel my cheeks go red. 'I know that – but,' I take a deep breath, 'do you really think she can hear us?'

Corinne shrugs, as she moves onto Lottie's right hand. 'No reason to think she can't, is there? I talk to my patients all day, even the ones who can't talk back – mostly because I think if I was in their position, I'd want someone to acknowledge me and be considerate in that way.'

I nod my head, and then focus on Corinne gently lifting Lottie's hands and slicking them with cream. I'm almost in a trance as I say, 'It's like I'm a little kid again, not sure if she's real or not. Expecting that any minute now she'll talk back to me . . .'

I blink and lift my eyes to find Corinne's are already on me, and she nods gently – encouraging me to go on.

I shrug. 'When I was little and I'd see Lottie on the TV, I used to think she was real. I thought it was like a phone call, and if I just waved enough or pulled silly faces or did a ridiculous dance, she'd look at me through the screen and acknowledge me, wave, smile – *something*.'

'That must have been very strange, growing up and seeing someone everywhere but not being able to talk to them. Very odd thing for a kid to wrap their head around.'

I nod. 'It took a while for me to grow out of it and realise what was real and what was Lottie playing make-believe on the TV . . . I feel like I'm back there though. Seeing and speaking to her, waiting for her to acknowledge me. Waiting for it all to be real again.'

For a little while we're quiet together, just sitting here listening to terrible Rhett Butler telling Scarlett O'Hara she's no lady.

'So, what else did you end up talking to Lottie about just now? If you don't mind my asking?'

I fidget a little in the seat. 'It probably wasn't appropriate . . .'

'Oh? Even better!' Corinne says, her voice a light bell trying to lift the mood.

I laugh. 'I was saying how I maybe might have met someone, a girl that I maybe might like.'

Corinne smiles. 'What's inappropriate about that?'

I shrug. 'It's complicated, but it also just feels wrong – possibly developing a minor crush on someone while all this is happening.' I gesture to Lottie lying there, one hand in Corinne's and her chest rising and falling slowly. 'The timing feels slightly off – wouldn't you agree?'

'Well, the movies would have us believe that fate rarely has a precise timetable for these things,' she says, glancing at the television.

I crinkle my brow and say, 'Life is nothing like the movies.'

'True,' Corinne says, and muses on it for a little while longer, then raises her eyebrows at me. 'Imagine if Lottie *could* talk back, what do you think she'd say?'

I feel myself frown, and then shrug as I delicately explain. 'We kind of met *because* of Lottie. And, I mean – my *bubbe* went through four husbands in her time . . .'

Corinne's hands glide along Lottie's as she finishes, and she folds them back neatly atop her chest, 'Well, there you go. Maybe this is all her way of telling you to take a chance on people?' She rises from her chair and begins gathering her things to move on to the next room and patient.

Heavy instrumental music swells from the TV as Scarlett O'Hara's melodrama continues to play out. And even though it's not the current scene, Corinne nods at the screen as she leaves. 'You know, tomorrow isn't guaranteed to be another day – not for everyone.'

And from where I'm sitting, it's hard to refute this fact.

SEVENTEEN

After I do changeover with Poe at the hospital, I find myself turning left instead of right. I walk along Argyle Street instead of taking Collins, and walk the twenty minutes or so back to North Hobart and the State Cinema.

It's just gone 1 p.m., and assuming Riya's at school, I realise I'll have some time to kill so I pop into the State Bookstore next door.

It's a long store with walls of high shelves filled gloriously with books and hanging glass bulbs lighting the way. In the middle are tables of book displays, and even though it's blessedly quiet, there are quite a few customers in the store and I join them in browsing contemplation.

I find myself drawn down the very back and to a wall of classics. Scanning the shelves for one title in particular, I find *Frankenstein.* I pull it down and begin reading.

You will rejoice to hear that no disaster has accompanied the commencement of an enterprise which you have regarded with such evil forebodings . . .

After purchasing the copy, I decide that maybe I can kill even more time seeing a film, so I head next door and line up at the box office. I'm completely overwhelmed to be called up next by Riya herself, smiling broadly at me and with two silver bats stuck to her collar-tips.

'I thought you were at school!'

Riya blinks and looks a bit taken aback at these being the first words out of my mouth, which I realise maybe didn't come out the way I intended.

'Half day. Were you hoping to avoid me?'

'What? No!' I hurriedly tear open the little brown paper bag I have in my hands, and show her the book I just purchased.

Her eyes light up, and she puts her hand out so I pass her the book. It's got a blue cover with an eye in the middle, and the title and Mary Shelley's name are all white and jagged, like teeth.

In an attempt to recover slightly and come across a modicum cooler, I say, 'I was kind of hoping this means we could be friends?'

And I think Riya blushes, as she hands the book back to me with a nod. 'Friends? Friends would be good . . .' Then she pauses, and I wonder if I should say something else. But then the moment passes when Riya says she can't hang out, as her shift doesn't end until five.

'Oh, I can come back another day then.'

She shakes her head. 'Or we could start your horror tutorial now?'

'Now?'

'Sure – that *is* why you're here?'

Again, it feels like she's waiting for me to say something else – but before I can wrap my head around it, or get my tongue to work, she's already speaking again. 'I still have *A Girl Walks Home Alone at Night* from our August club. If you like, I can put it on for you in one of the basement cinemas? We don't screen there during the day except in school holidays.'

When I say that would be great, Riya turns to one of her colleagues and asks him to take over tickets for a bit. I follow her once more down the stairs and to the cellar cinemas.

'So, what's this film about?'

Riya ducks behind the screen for a bit, and then remerges to tell me. 'It's a vampire movie written and directed by Ana Lily Amirpour.'

'Vampires? Should I really be watching this by myself in a basement . . . ?'

Riya laughs. 'Relax, it's been called "the first Iranian vampire Western", and it's more stylish and retro-cool than out and out horrifyingly scary, even though it has its moments.' Then she smiles at me. 'I think you can handle it.'

And I do. It's a bizarrely beautiful black and white movie about a skateboarding vampire heroine, who wears a chador like a cape and stalks a town called Bad City. She meets this guy and invites him back to her apartment, where they listen to vinyl and she manages to resist his exposed neck.

It's almost more of a silent movie for how little dialogue there is. I'm a little surprised when Riya pops back in once the credits are rolling, takes a seat on the couch with me and says her favourite thing in the movie is the sound and soundtrack.

'Really? But it's so quiet . . .'

'Exactly! It makes the music and sound so much bigger.'

'What do you mean?'

'Before she was writing and directing, Amirpour was a singer and bassist in a rock band so of course the soundtrack is a total kaleidoscope of sound that also reflects the mish-mash genres of the film itself . . .'

As Riya talks, her eyes light up. Maybe that sounds cliché and biologically impossible, especially considering we're sitting in a dim basement. But honestly – she gets a glow from within as she starts talking.

'. . . it's a little Spaghetti Western, 1960s groovy with Jean-Luc Godard influences, and stuck somewhere between the nineteenth and twenty-first centuries. There's a ton of music from Bei Ru – this very cool Armenian-American music producer who mixes everything with Middle Eastern rhythms. Not to mention the Persian and alternative rock of bands like Radio Tehran . . .'

I smile and nod, and I hope I don't seem disinterested – because I'm not! Even as all these names and influences she's citing wash over me, I keep crashing against the joy in her eyes. Something in them reminds me of . . . well – *me*. The way I used to talk after a day at the Hobart Children's Theatre Company, explaining to Lottie, my parents and Yael about blocking and staging, and exactly how I'd be delivering my lines and why that mattered to the story and, and, and – a child's ability to go on and on with such glee.

Riya does too, getting so excited at this point that she stands a little in her seat so she can tuck a leg underneath herself. 'But then she'll throw in some post-punk from England with White Lies during a romance sequence that plays just a little too long to drag the moment out!' Riya's hands are moving now too, waving as she adds, 'Plus, the sheer *genius* of getting sound designer Alan Splet – known for his David Lynch collaborations – to have howling wind and the rolling creak of tumbleweeds throughout! Truly inspiring.'

I realise I've been so focused on Riya's lips, the way she quickly licked them as she was talking and the dimple they pulled, like on a string, that when they stop moving to half-smile at me, I realise my own jaw must be on the floor.

Riya blushes and hastily tucks an escaped curl behind her ear again. 'What? Music and composing are kind of my thing.'

'They are?'

Riya nods. 'Oh yeah. I play piano, guitar and have been known to occasionally sing. I've even applied to study Screen Music at the Australian Film Television and Radio School.'

'That's in Sydney, right?'

She nods and I suddenly get this flash of Yael in my mind. I picture her raising an eyebrow at me, and saying 'See? What have I been telling you!'

'I mean, I might not get in but AFTRS is definitely the dream.' Riya pronounces the acronym *afters*, and then turns to me. 'What about you?'

The hair on the back of my neck pricks up. 'What about me?'

'Where are you going to school while you're here?'

'Actually, I've very technically already graduated.'

'Really?'

I nod. 'Yeah, it's long and boring and complicated,' I try deflecting.

'Okay, so – what's next then?'

I nearly blurt out that I'm just trying to get through Lottie dying. That I can't think much more beyond that, even though I've been unable to envision my future even before she got sick.

And I'm a little shocked to realise that there's a part of me that wants to confide in Riya, how grief feels a little like emotional jetlag right now – compounded by anger I've still got leftover for Lottie, which then leads to guilt . . . so my whole body has this bone-deep weariness to it.

But instead I shrug, and say I'm not sure – I'm still figuring it out.

'You wouldn't want to try acting again?'

'Ah, no – not that.'

I wait, scared that she'll follow up with some – what did Yael call it? – fangirling. It's a reminder that she's seen me at my most hated and vulnerable, and I don't know what I'll do if she presses the point or shows me that she's more interested in the *idea* of me than the person sitting right in front of her.

'Do you like yum cha?'

I blink at the question. 'Yum cha?'

'Delicious Cantonese brunch?'

'Um, yes – yes, I like yum cha.'

'Cool, would you maybe want to grab some with me? There's this great little place at The Cat & Fiddle Arcade – and my shift ends in half an hour.'

Just as I'm wondering if this could possibly be construed as an invitation for a date, Riya follows up by saying, 'We could continue your feminist horror tutorial and talk some more about Ana Lily Amirpour?'

And all I can say is, 'Sure.'

Not a date then, and I let the little bite of disappointment sink in.

EIGHTEEN

It's three days later when Mum finds me watching Lottie lop off some undead guy's head with a cricket bat.

The theatre room is on the third floor of the converted attic. There's a DVD projector hanging from a beam, and a big white screen that automatically comes down when you hit a button. It's carpeted up here and the three couches and armrests are all velvet and plush to aid noise-reduction.

'Ellie – what on earth are you doing?'

I aim the DVD remote at the projector up ahead and pause the scene, just as a much younger Lottie is swinging the bat and right at the moment of impact so there's a little bit of garish syrup-red blood on the screen.

I wonder if I should tell Mum that I'm undergoing a horror-cinema education, but decide better of it. I'm unsure how I'd broach the topic of Riya and how we met because of Lottie, or even how to explain that I'm partly watching this film in pursuit of a crush that's really inappropriate right now considering I'm in early mourning.

So instead I say, 'I thought it was time I watched this one.'

'You did?'

'Yeah – I've seen most of Lottie's other films. I figured it was time to delve into the vault and drag this one out.'

Mum still looks unconvinced, so I change tack and ask if she's ever seen it.

She comes fully into the room then. She takes a seat beside me on the purple velvet couch and sinks down. She grabs a teal silk pillow and holds it to her middle as she smiles at the screen. 'Actually, the first time I saw it was with your dad.'

'Really?'

She nods. 'Yeah, at a rooftop cinema in Melbourne. I think it was our third or fourth date? He'd bought us tickets to this old movie screening, not realising my mother would be in it, and he was *so* horrified. He kept apologising and saying he didn't know and we could go if I wanted to.'

'But you didn't?'

Mum shakes her head. 'No, he felt so bad already and I told him, honestly I'd never seen it.'

I turn my body towards her and lean an arm on the back of the couch, holding my head in one hand. 'How was it?'

'Ah, I think I was more terrified by my mother's bum cheeks in those hot-pants on an eighteen-foot screen than I was by the undead zombie things.' I laugh, and she adds, 'But it was okay and your dad got lucky that night, so I wasn't too traumatised.'

'Mum!'

I settle back on the couch, leaning into a corner now and press play again, since there's only a few minutes left on this first instalment anyway.

It's the scene Corinne told me about last week of Lottie's character Hannah-Jane and Ryan Longford as her husband Marty, getting up on the roof of their kid's primary school and looking out at all the little lights of their town twinkling in the distance.

It's an oddly beautiful scene, considering there's bits of brains on the cricket bat Lottie brings to rest on her shoulder, and because the dead are still rising down below. There's definitely a sense of this being just the beginning of a terrible apocalypse – but for now, Hannah-Jane and Marty are safe and they have a plan and they're just admiring everything they've lost, even though from far away it all looks just the same.

The screen goes blank just as you start to hear the shuffling, groaning noise of those creatures – and the sound of Marty and Hannah-Jane's shoes scuffling on the roof, about to meet the monsters again.

'What did *you* think of it?' Mum asks, as the credits roll.

'It was . . . okay. But – does Marty die in the next one?'

'How do you know that? He literally dies in the first fifteen minutes of *The Hazards II* and it was one of the biggest twists in cinema! Up there with Hitchcock killing off Janet Leigh at the beginning of *Psycho*!'

I shrug but don't feel like going into how I know she's meant to be a final girl after all, which suggests going it alone. 'Just a good guess.'

'Okay, well – if you're quite done with the movie marathon, your uncle Tobin is due a change-over at the hospital and it's down to you or Poe.'

'I can go.'

Mum turns to leave, but before she does, I ask, 'Have you spoken to him, lately?'

Mum stops and looks back at me. 'I'm about to go and tell him you're heading down, why?'

'No, I mean have you *spoken* to him – deep and meaningfuls, or anything?'

Mum crosses her arms and sighs. 'About what, Ellie?'

I jump up from the couch and go to take the DVD out, still talking as I do. 'I think you've always had the wrong idea about Lottie and Poe, and when they got together . . .'

'Ellie, I'm not in the mood.'

'No, seriously – Poe all but told me that nothing happened while Harvey was alive!'

'This is none of your business . . .'

'Of course it is! Poe is like your father and most times you can't even stand to be in the same room as him.'

'Poe is not my father, Ellie.'

'Mum –'

'No! You have no right to go delving into what is better left unsaid.'

'Unsaid? Mum – you really don't think this is a final concern that Lottie would want fixed, between you and him?'

'You are in no position to talk about what Lottie would want.'

'What does that mean?'

Mum's jaw is clenched and her arms still crossed. 'Ellie, are you really going to stand there and accuse me of weaponising silence when you did the same to your grandmother, all this time?' she says.

I feel it like a punch to the gut, like the wind has been knocked out of me. 'Are you serious?'

Mum shakes her head. 'What do you want me to say, Ellie? I didn't speak to my own mother for a year after what she did to you, but I had to forgive her. She apologised and atoned and I couldn't go on missing her . . .'

I feel my breath quicken and my heart beats loudly, echoing in my ears and I latch onto those words. 'Apologise and atone? *Really*? She knew what they did to me was wrong and she let it happen anyway . . .'

Before I can go on, Mum raises her hands in pleading. 'She thought they were getting the best out of you, *helping* you. She said it was like method acting, Ellie. She didn't know how much they'd frighten and use you, and you didn't tell her!'

I can feel the tears coming now, running hot down my cheeks and salting my lips. 'I wanted to please her! I wanted her to be proud of me, to see that I could . . .' And then I shake my head, because this is exactly the merry-go-round argument I'd get into a screaming match with Lottie over. She was sorry, immediately followed by all the reasons she really didn't have to be – all the ways she wasn't really at fault and I was overreacting or misremembering or didn't understand this side of the business *or or or*. And now I can't quite believe that after all this time, my own mother is now repeating the lines back to me.

'I was a kid! I was eleven. It shouldn't have been up to me to save myself, when I didn't even know I could speak up and tell them no!'

I'm shouting, but I don't even know if she can hear me – Lottie certainly refused to.

I pull the sleeves of my skivvy down over my hands and use them to wipe my eyes. I take a deep breath and try to control my voice to at least get the next words out clearly. 'Get Poe to go to the hospital instead of me.'

I don't know if Mum tries to say anything after that or if she calls out to me. There's a ringing in my ears and then I'm pounding down the stairs to my blue room, slamming the door behind me. Without thinking too much I pull on jeans, a warm green turtleneck knit and a long black duffle coat. I snatch up my backpack and black Converse shoes, and then I'm heading down again and out the front door.

NINETEEN

I walk around aimlessly for a bit, wandering Salamanca and the Pier. At some point, I get colder and open my backpack to see if I packed my gloves, when I crunch something and pull out the flyer and envelope for the film club from the other night.

I turn it over and am surprised to see Riya's name – Riya Vaidhyanathan – and her return address written down in bold handwriting, and find that she lives on Park Street in New Town.

And then I get an idea for where I'd rather be. And since it's a Thursday, and Riya doesn't work Thursdays, she should be home, given that it's just gone 5 p.m. For the first time in a long time I find myself regretting that I don't have active social media accounts, and that Riya doesn't either. I also wish we'd exchanged numbers at some point, so I could call or text her to ask. We just always seem to be talking too much to officially swap details.

Maybe this will be too weird, and a total overstep. But at the same time, I want to take the leap into distraction – like I can wash away the confrontation with Mum and thoughts of Lottie by plunging myself into Riya's path.

New Town is a little past the State Cinema, and for once I'm too exhausted to walk. I use my phone to organise a ride-share that comes almost immediately. And even though it's a ten-minute drive, I spend every one of those minutes as if I'm peeling petals in my mind: I should go, I shouldn't go, I should go, I shouldn't go, I should go . . . and then we're right outside a large building of what looks like four two-storey units. Each with a black roof and red bricks that make it look very '60s with a neat and abundant vegetable patch running the entire length of the front, only interrupted by a pathway to the doorway of each unit.

I get out of the car and double-check her address on the white envelope, confirming she's number four. I walk up the six or so steps to her front door, take a deep breath, and knock.

A short lady who must be her mother answers. I can tell the two are at least related because this woman has the same curly black hair that Riya does, even though it's currently up in a bun and I can see there's a few wispy white streaks in it.

'Yes? Can I help you?' she asks, smiling gently even as a small frown is also folding between her brows.

'Hi, yes – hello – I'm wondering if Riya is home?'

And I suddenly feel utterly ridiculous to realise I've never done this before. Randomly knocking on someone's door and asking if their kid can come out and play? Surely, it's the reason texting was even invented, to avoid the very awkwardness of this.

'Who is asking?'

'Oh, I'm Ellie Marsden! I know Riya! We know each other . . .' I swallow and make my smile bigger as I finish. 'I was just wondering if she's around?'

'Maa, who is it?'

The voice comes from up the stairs just behind the woman, and then a pair of bare feet and legs clad in stripey black and white tights appear at the top of the stairs.

The woman leaves the front door to stand at the bottom of the stairs. She looks up, and says, 'Friend of yours – Ellie?'

And I swear I think I see the toes suddenly go rigid in surprise, before the striped legs come bounding down the bright-orange carpeted stairs and Riya appears – hair out and wild.

'Hi!' she says

'Hello,' I reply.

She's standing on the last step and I'm at the door, her mother looking between us and smiling, slightly.

It's Riya who snaps out of it first. 'Maa – this is Ellie, she's from film club.'

Not a lie, but not entirely true either.

'Ellie, nice to meet you. I'm Brinda,' the woman says.

And then there's silence, and I feel the need to explain myself slightly. 'I was just wanting to see if you can hang out for a little while?'

Brinda and Riya look at each other, and I get the feeling they're having a whole conversation using just their eyes and eyebrows, but it's Brinda who breaks the silence first. 'Have you done all your study?'

Riya nods.

'You sure?'

'*Ji ji!* I promise. Can Ellie stay for a bit? It's too cold to hang outside.'

After a moment, Brinda relents. 'Not too late though, understand?'

Riya waves her hand, yes.

Brinda gets me through the front door and takes my duffle coat to hang up on a rack. I remove my Converse shoes and I notice Riya motioning with her head for her mum to leave. And sure enough, when I turn around Brinda is all but giggling and waving her hands as though to say *okay, okay I'm going*!

'It was nice to meet you, Ms Vaidhyanathan,' I say, and she smiles even wider – and I can see where Riya gets it from.

'And you, Ellie.'

Then I'm following Riya up the stairs where there are three white doors. Riya leads me through one of them. We enter her bedroom, which is a little much to take in all at once, so instead I focus on her for a second, and exactly what she's wearing as we're standing together in the centre of the room.

She's in pyjamas. They are *Wizard of Oz* themed, which explains the black and white striped tights, just like the Witch of the East's curled under Dorothy's house. The oversized white t-shirt that hangs nearly to her knees features an image of Judy Garland's Dorothy, skipping arm-in-arm with Diana Ross from *The Wiz*, with the two famous Toto terriers running alongside their respective Dorothys.

It definitely isn't trademarked but it is still very cool.

And at least it gives me the idea of breaking this weird silence by humming a few bars from the famous song in *The Wiz* and I watch Riya's eyes light up.

'Wait – how are you even here right now?'

I reach into my back pocket and hold up the folded envelope. Her envelope – the one she'd sent to Lottie. 'Return address.'

'Okay, that's very *Harriet the Spy* of you.' And then Riya turns around to hastily start closing and clearing textbooks from her bed.

While Riya clears space, I take a moment to fully take in her room, by turning in a slow circle. One side has a double-hung window that looks out onto Park Street, with a wide enough ledge for the turntable that sits there. She has a double bed, a free-standing white wardrobe, and in one corner sits a Yamaha keyboard and an acoustic guitar on a stand.

There are artfully arranged posters on the wall opposite her bed, while on the floor are DVDs, cassettes, vinyl records and books lined up on makeshift shelves made from planks of wood and standing bricks.

I move closer to admire the posters, and I recognise one of them, even without the *Bride of Frankenstein* electrode title. She's pretty iconic with high hair and lightning strips of white down either side, her bandaged arms out rigid in front of her, dark lips and slashed black brows.

Next along is a movie I vaguely recognise from a few years ago, called *Jennifer's Body*. The poster is of this beautiful woman, Megan Fox – with legs for days – dressed in a school uniform and sitting at a school table. The only thing that gives the horror away is a trickle of blood in the corner of her mouth, and the dismembered body part sticking out of her backpack on the ground.

'One of my favourites,' Riya calls over her shoulder, seeing me staring.

'I can guess why.'

'Oh come on, a little more credit please,' she says, and when I turn to her I see she's smiling at me. 'Plenty of people would have been lured into the movie by Megan Fox and the way she's been criminally typecast in everything else, only to be subjected to a movie of female rage and gory revenge. It's honestly brilliant, and it deserved way more attention when it first came out.'

And once again I'm in awe of her, and my jaw must reflect that. But to cover slightly while she goes back to cleaning up her textbooks I say, 'Okay, that sounded like an essay.'

Riya throws me a smile over her shoulder. 'I may have submitted something similar to my Rotten Tomatoes account.'

I move on to the next poster. This one I'm definitely not familiar with, and it looks like something from the 1940s era. A beautiful woman with a heart-shaped hairdo is peering around a grandfather clock about to strike midnight. She has red nails like claws and a pretty terribly drawn big cat hovering above her head. I read the quote underneath the title: *She was one of the dreaded Cat People doomed to prowl by night . . . a snarling, clawing KILLER!*

'Is this a real film?' I ask.

Riya turns to double-check the one I'm pointing to. '*Cat People*?' When she looks back at me her eyes are sparkling. 'Oh, yeah and it's amazing! About this Serbian woman who's running from an ancient family curse that will see her turn into a bloodthirsty panther if she ever experiences a sexual encounter.'

I make a noise, somewhere between disbelief and impressed, and Riya laughs. 'Oh yeah, you have no idea! It's totally a film exploring women's sexuality and how it's constantly caged, for fear of what would happen if it was ever fed.'

'Ah, subtext meets subtlety I see . . .'

'Well, yeah – it's addressing the very purpose of myth and legend, the whole point of stories for a really long time was to keep women in check. Like fairy tales.'

'Fairy tales are about not letting blood-lusty panthers loose as a metaphor for women's sexual desire?'

She laughs. 'No – not that literal, at least not all of them – but the point of fables and fairy tales was to mostly keep young women in line. Hello? *Goldilocks and the Three Bears* is literally telling young, curious women not to go jumping into strangers' beds. The Brothers Grimm were passing down tales to keep ladies in check, and fairy tales were really the original horror stories.'

I nod along because actually that makes a weird amount of sense.

'There is usually a final girl at the end of fairy tales.' I turn around as I say this to find Riya beaming at me, and I notice that her bed is clear and she's perched on the edge, looking at me, so I move to sit cross-legged on the floor.

'Did you come here just to get a brief horror lesson and movie recommendations?'

I laugh. 'No, that was just a bonus.' I start folding the hem of my jumper. 'I actually had a fight with my mum tonight, and just needed to get out of the house.'

'Ellie, I'm so sorry. Is everything okay?'

I can't bring myself to nod and force a smile and pretend like it is. So I don't. Instead I shrug and cast my eyes down, focusing on the accordion fold I'm making of my hem.

'Can I ask what the fight was about?' Riya prods, gently.

And I really want to tell her. About Lottie and me, the movie that broke us, but that Riya loves so much. Not to mention how complicated it is that I still can't forgive my grandmother, even as she lies dying . . . the layers and layers of explanation I have to unwind exhaust me, so I pick one that's easier just to save myself some grief. 'Actually, it was about my grandmother.'

'Oh no, I hope she's okay?'

I almost cry, right then – from bursting to tell this girl everything – but knowing that I can't.

'She's in rehab, and she's all right,' I lie, 'but it wasn't about that. It was kind of about this really old fight we've been having for a few years now. Also linked to why I left Hobart and haven't been home in a while.'

When I say this, Riya's brow creases and she bites her bottom lip. 'Ellie, about that – I think I kind of know what you're talking about.'

I snap my eyes up. 'You do?'

She nods, and my heart beats fast and my breathing shallows as she continues. 'I go to Ogilvie Girls, but we even heard about what happened to you at Queen Street School when you went there. It was kind of an awful local legend, and I'm so sorry.'

My hands start to sweat and I can feel the red creep going up my neck. I feel a combination of light-headed relief that she doesn't know the extent of what happened on set (because how could she?), but a bone-deep dread that she's going to detail what came after, when the movie was released.

'I think it was just awful, the way they hounded you out of the place and all those parents got involved.'

I see bursts of black behind my eyes when I close them, and I clench my fists against the beating in my chest.

'Ellie? Ellie – are you . . .'

I feel a hand fold over my fist, and I concentrate on the coolness of her skin and the smell of citrus that's stronger because her hair's out.

'Count to five, Ellie – just count with me,' she says, softly.

It happened in Year 7, only a couple of months into first term. I guess some of the students didn't like that I went to their school, or they thought I was stuck-up or something. I don't know. It started with them just filming me on their phones, waiting at the canteen, eating lunch by myself or else with Yael and her friends on the oval. I'd look up and at first, I'd thought I was crazy and Yael did too. It was only one or two of them then, and they'd try and hide it. But I could swear I felt them watching me, filming me.

'One.'

I blew up at a bunch of these boys one day. They had followed me and filmed me walking home. I stopped in the middle of the street and begged them to stop, then I ran home. The next day I found out they'd taken the footage of me and done something with it, cut it with my part in the movie. Me in school uniform on the street, screaming at them to just leave me alone – and then video of me from *Blood & Jacaranda*, my character's dead-eyed face screaming with a mouthful of prosthetic fangs . . . well, they sent that all around.

'Two.'

And then everyone seemed to get in on it. I'd be walking at the bottom of the science block, stop, and look up – and hanging over the balcony would be these seniors with their phones out, filming me. Trying to – I don't know? Make me angry or upset? I'd ask them to stop, and they'd say something ridiculous like 'It's a free country, and we can film anybody' . . . I think they wanted me to pull the 'I'm a celebrity' card or something.

'Three.'

I didn't. Tell anyone, I mean. I didn't want to give them the satisfaction of thinking they'd got to me. Even though I started staying home from school, faking cramps and stomach flu. Eating my lunch in an empty classroom when I did have to go. And then somebody leaked the videos, or else passed them on deliberately to that gossip website, and then other media picked it up. 'Star of *Blood & Jacaranda* Bullied', and 'Lottie Lovinger's Granddaughter Living Hellish School Life' . . .

'Four.'

The school found out who did it. It wasn't hard. They were pretty proud of themselves . . . I think there was about five of them in the end, even though the whole school was probably in on it, or at least it felt that way to me. They got suspended for two weeks while the school conducted an investigation, and there was talk of further action, maybe expulsion, for what was basically stalking and harassment – and my parents were so angry. But then the students' parents got involved and said they didn't deserve any punishment. They said their kids didn't really understand what they were doing. They were just starstruck and didn't know how to show their admiration for me. So much bullshit.

'Five.'

In the end, the school recommended that I might feel more comfortable in a different environment. And by then, I was more than happy to leave. Dad deliberately took a job in

London to get me away and give me some time and distance, I guess. But it just didn't stop, the ways that film ruined my life.

'Five, Ellie – *five.*'

I open my eyes to find that I am holding Riya's hands, and she's sitting cross-legged in front of me, her face so close to mine. And I suddenly flash back to *A Girl Walks Home Alone at Night* – and this one really close-up shot of The Girl and Arash listening to a long punk song and just staring at one another. Their faces so close.

'I could be a vampire.'

Riya blinks at me. 'What?'

'You've only ever seen me at night, never during the day.'

Riya's mouth kicks up in a smile, one that brings out the dimple in her left cheek. 'Actually, you're right,' she says.

I squeeze her hand once and let go. I clear my throat and then look just over her shoulder, to all the horror paraphernalia. 'Why aren't you scared of me?' I ask.

'What do you mean?' She frowns.

I lift a hand to my face, and without touching it I make a swipe motion to indicate all of it. 'I've been turned into figurines and Halloween costumes. Ah-Pei the other day literally told me I once gave her nightmares . . .' Riya starts shaking her head to contest that point, but I wave her down gently and go on. 'I know it's ridiculous, and I don't look the same now as I did when I was eleven and full of make-up and werewolf prosthetics, but I have all these reminders of that movie following me around and sometimes people can't see past it to who I am now . . . but you can?'

What I don't add is how Lottie couldn't see me either. Couldn't see me at 12 and 13, still struggling with the legacy of that movie and the way it continued to hurt me. She took the side of the parents at my old school, told me to consider that maybe my fellow students really were my biggest fans and just didn't know how to show me . . . and I was so angry. Everything came bubbling back to the surface – the filming and the aftermath, and yet another way that Lottie found to discredit me. I went away to London with my parents, as much to start afresh as to get away from Lottie – and everything changed, after that.

I realise I haven't said anything for a while now, that we've been sitting here in silence. 'I wish I could skateboard right now.'

And Riya blinks again, like I'm giving her whiplash. 'What?'

'Like that vampire girl in the movie, how she tools around Bad Town on her skateboard? She makes it look really peaceful and badass.'

Riya waits a beat, holds my eye and then gives a nod and a smile – as if to let me know that she's willing to let me off the conversational hook, *this time*. 'I could pop next door and see if Arin has one? He went through a real "Sk8er Boi" phase.'

I breathe a sigh of relief that we're drifting further away from the topics we've been discussing, and so I keep propelling us forward. 'Your cousin Arin lives next door?'

'Yup, it's me, my maa and pitah – that's Dad – and normally my brother, but he's gone off to uni on the mainland. Then my aunt and uncle have the apartment next to ours with Arin, another cousin and her husband, and my dādī and dādā – my grandparents – are two doors down,' she says.

And maybe to anyone else that would all sound like *a lot*, but I come from Lovinger House, where it's entirely normal to have multiple generations and branches of the family tree living under one roof at any given time.

'I should still probably get going – even without a skateboard to get me home.'

'Are you sure?'

'Yeah, totally. I had my little breakdown, now I'm good to go.'

'Ellie!'

'I'm okay, really.' I breathe deeply and smile, just to show her.

'Do you need a ride, or –'

'No, no – I actually got a ride-share today, I'm all good. I'll order a car now.'

After I do, I thrust my phone at her and ask for her number. 'So maybe we can arrange to meet in daylight?' She smiles and obliges, then goes to her bedside table and passes her phone to me, so I can do the same.

'And make sure you text me when you get home safe, okay?' she says.

When I hand her phone back, Riya's staring at me a little funnily and I wipe self-consciously at my face. 'Do I have snot, or what?'

'No, no I just realised – you look a lot like Simone Simon.'

I turn around and see that I'm standing right in front of the *Cat People* poster, but I'm sure I look nothing like her the actor with her heart-shaped hair and long red nails.

'My dādā had this box of old VHS movies when I was growing up, and *Cat People* was one of them. I used to watch it so much I wore the tape out, and my pitah bought me that poster to cheer me up.' Riya tucks another strand of hair behind her ear, looks down at the ground and her bare foot, before meeting my eyes again to say. 'I guess she was technically another of my first crushes.'

I don't know what to say to that, but my body sways a little towards her and I swear Riya's eyes flicker down to my lips, and right when I think I could close the distance between us, my phone dings.

'Your car is here.'

And all I can think as I go down the stairs, say goodnight to Brinda and pull on my coat is how badly I want another chance. Another shot at the scene in Riya's room and a different ending – but instead of a film slate clapping a new take, it's the slam of the car door once I get in and pull away from her house, turning in the back seat to see the glow from her first-storey window that eventually fades as I get further away.

TWENTY

If grief feels like emotional jetlag, then waiting as someone slowly dies and fades away is like being in a perpetual airport terminal – waiting and waiting for someone else's flight to depart, a limbo that pressurises time until it has no meaning. I've only been home in Hobart for two weeks, but it's starting to feel like another lifetime entirely.

The added strain of not talking to my mum after I got home that night and into the next day made everything feel even more undone and unusual.

The uncles and Poe can feel it but are wise to stay out of our way and not offer commentary. Even Dad – who has been filled in from both our sides – gently walked around the topic when on the phone to me, which probably means he's brainstorming how to tackle it from another direction.

And then late in the afternoon when I'm all the way at the back of the house in the conservatory reading *The Big Issue*, I hear music.

I sit up from where I'm lying on the leather couch and look out to the garden – where I think the music is coming from – but the yellow wattle trees stare back unknowing, and I stand up to follow the tune.

I wander back into the house and the noise gets a little louder as I walk down the hallway and through the kitchen, where Poe is sitting at the counter drinking tea and studiously avoiding looking at me.

'You can hear that, right?' I ask, but he comically shrugs in nonchalance and I walk on towards the front door, where I realise it's definitely coming from above my head and in the vicinity of the library one floor up.

I also realise the song that's playing is Thelma Plum's bluesy beat 'Homecoming Queen', and just as I turn around to start climbing the staircase and follow the sound, I stop dead in my tracks to look up and see Yael standing at the top, waiting for me.

My cousin's smile is as wide as her arms which are spread so I can appreciate the full effect of the long burgundy velvet robe with lace-trim edges and winged sleeves that she's sporting. She looks like a Mae West throwback but dressed in black tracksuit pants, pink slippers and an Ivy Park black jumper underneath.

I start slowly climbing the staircase, and Yael drops her arms to clasp her hands in front of her chest and in an almost painfully accurate Lottie impersonation, she bellows at me, 'My *darling*, you could give Jean Seberg a run for her money!'

I self-consciously run a hand through my shaggy short hair, until I come to stand one step down from Yael who cups my face in her cool hands.

'Is this a good surprise, or a bad surprise?' she asks.

'That depends . . .' I begin. 'What are you doing here?'

Yael lifts her hands from my face, and one of them delves into a deep pocket of the velvet robe. It smells a little musty and has no doubt been found buried in the back of an ancestor's closet somewhere. She plucks her phone from the pocket, taps the screen and the music stops.

'Was she good-surprised?' Poe calls, through the wind-tunnel of the hallway from where he's still situated in the kitchen.

Yael walks to the railing and leans over, enough that I bound the final stair and stand behind her, one hand clasping her velvet-clad shoulder just in case.

'Remains to be seen!' she shouts down below.

Yael pulls back and I let out a sigh of relief, but then she's hooking her arm through mine so our elbows are linked.

'Come on,' she says. 'It's time for a roof-walk and talk . . .'

And we start padding along the carpeted hallway – both of us in our slippers – to the little door at the end, that reveals a narrow spiral staircase leading to the widow's walk of the roof.

It's a railed rooftop platform that sits atop our house and a little awkwardly, I might add. That's because one of the great-uncles had it added on some time in the 1940s, when they were all the rage of coastal architecture out of America. The Lovingers never quite knew what to do with it, though, until someone bought a telescope to sit there seasonally and give the place an air of scientific endeavour, at least – until Yael and I turned it into our childhood hideaway.

Maybe most adults wouldn't think it a great idea to let an eight-year-old and a nine-and-a-half-year-old lug sheets and pillows onto the top of a roof, with only an enclosed cupola for safety, and timber railing all around . . . but we found that when our parents were working during the day, and Lottie wasn't away on a set somewhere, she was rarely inclined to act like most adults.

Lottie delighted in us hiding away up here to eat Vegemite and cheese sandwiches, or chocolate babka, and turn the place into the Tower of London in our imaginations. Lottie liked it even more when she got to play the character of Rapunzel's stepmother captor, or Henry VIII come to farewell one of his soon-to-be headless wives as a guise to come check on us every hour or so.

Lottie would always choose imagination over practicality any day. And she was one of those rare adults who trusted children to be ultimately sensible and rise to the occasion of her belief in us. Maybe a little too much.

I'm thinking about that as Yael pushes open the trapdoor leading to the widow's walk and hoists herself up the last of the stairs to reach the top. I soon join her and we both take a turn around the platform to admire the view of Hobart that's all around. The mountain and river, little houses of our town and cars gliding by . . . I'm so caught up I don't even bother to check my wristwatch to see if we're about to be spotted by the tourist bus who could surely see us. The perfect sky is blue and there's a chill in the air but with the sun on us, we can barely shiver from it.

Eventually, though, I need to sit down by leaning against the railing so the sun is behind me and not in my eyes. But of course, Yael instead plucks a pair of Ray-Ban sunglasses from within another pocket of the robe, pops them on her face. She lies down flat beside me with her head near my hip so she can soak up the sun.

'If you're quite ready,' I say, a hint of amusement in my voice. 'Your dad called me.'

Ah. So he did find a new direction.

'Oh,' is all I can think to reply.

Yael shrugs. 'Yeah, but I had also been thinking that my place is here, and uni is giving me leeway with my exams on compassionate grounds. So it all worked out.'

I stretch my legs out in front of me. 'So what did he tell you? What do you know?'

Yael replies by heaving herself up and sitting next to me, so her back is against the railing now too. She makes a big show of arranging the burgundy velvet robe around her so it fans out before explaining. 'He said you and Aunt Louise had an all-out blue, and it was about what you went through, on the film set.'

I nod my head.

'Do you want to talk about it?' she asks softly.

And something that's been boiling beneath my surface for a couple of days now erupts, so I snap back, 'Do you want me to? You've never been interested in hearing my side of things before, not really.'

And I'm surprised when Yael doesn't snipe back, but instead says, 'That's true.'

Her reply immediately deflates me; there's nowhere for my anger to go.

'I was jealous of you, you know.' As she says this, Yael removes her sunglasses so she can look over at me. 'When we were little and playing dress-ups, I was just goofing around, but you – *you* became a different person. It was so weird, Ellie – how seriously you took it, and how much you could disappear.'

I laugh at the memories. 'You used to say, "Be you now, Ellie. Be you."'

Yael nods. 'One day I got all sad and pissy about it because you were off play-acting when I was ready to be done, and Lottie found me and said I just had to accept that you had the bug. She said your parents knew it; she knew it. That was around the time you joined the Kids' Theatre, and I suddenly saw that everyone was looking at you in this new way . . .'

'Looking how?'

'Like you were carrying on the Lovinger legacy.' She rolls her eyes and a smile stretches her mouth, but it doesn't reach her eyes. 'And then Lottie got you that movie role, and I thought, *That does it, she's officially the crown jewel in the family tree*!'

'Yeah well, trust me – everyone looking at you like you're a performing monkey is no fun either. Or when they all have these expectations of who you're meant to be, because of your family. The branches of that tree are heavy, believe me.'

Yael frowns at me.

I look back. 'What?'

She shakes her head. 'Don't you get it? That's *why* I was jealous – they never looked at me like that, which is its own special kind of hurt.' Yael turns her head and looks out into the distance, towards kunanyi and the houses in between. 'Nobody outside the family ever saw me as a real-life Lovinger, just somebody playing dress-up. Why do you think I cave in and try so hard to look the part?' She flaps her velvet sleeves as she says this.

And I have to admit . . . I never thought of that. My uncle Jasper and aunt Constance adopted Yael when she was a baby, and a year later I was born and so we grew up together, firm cousins and best friends. Yael being adopted was never kept secret; it was just part of her history – her story.

'I never knew you felt that way about being adopted?' I nudge her shoulder and she nudges back. 'You were always so cool and above it all at school – smart *and* popular. I never knew you were so . . . insecure?'

At this Yael dramatically whips her Ray-Bans out again, pops them on her face and shrugs. 'Maybe I am a better actor than you gave me credit for,' she says before sighing again. 'It's just these thoughts and feelings come and go, sometimes. I love my parents, completely. I love our family . . . but sometimes I do think about tracking down my biological parents too, and maybe I will some day. It's just two thoughts existing side-by-side is all.'

It sounds so simple when she puts it like that. And I wonder if that's all I need: to accept that I love Lottie, and I'm still mad at her. Holding two of these emotions in my heart at the same time.

Before I can think more on it, Yael continues.

'But what I'm trying to say is we were both kids when you went through what you did, and maybe I didn't react *perfectly* because I was caught up in my own head – but at the same time I can understand *now* how wrong what happened to you was when you were young and vulnerable. I hope you can cut me some slack and see that I was just a kid too.'

She's right. We were thick as thieves growing up, and then I was eleven when I went off to do the film. I came back and everything was changed, slowly and then all at once. I'd tried telling her, and she knew what I went through at school – but it just now occurs to me that there's a whole other side to why she never seemed to want to listen.

'It didn't feel that way,' I say instead slowly. 'It felt like nobody wanted to hear all the ways that movie wrecked me, and how much I hated it. It was like they all wanted me to play a part and stop complaining, to keep acting even after the cameras stopped rolling.'

Yael nods. 'I didn't get that. I just thought you were throwing away everything you ever wanted and blaming Lottie for it not going your way.'

'Is that what she said?'

I'm curious. Mum was right the other day; she and my dad refused to speak to Lottie for a year after it was all out in the open, and I often wondered what the rest of the family were told during our absence.

'The most she ever said to me was that she regretted the sacrifices she'd made.'

'That makes sense.' I sigh. 'I do feel like she sacrificed me, our relationship – for some crappy film role . . .' I shake my head. 'I feel like you did when we were little kids; *be you now, be you.* I feel like I'm still trying to figure out all these sides to Lottie, and I want her to somehow tell me which one was real. The grandmother who let us come and play up here, blasting Idina Menzel and Aretha Franklin down below . . . or the one who threw me to the wolves for some asshole director's vision.'

Or is it like Yael said: can all these parts of Lottie exist, all at once?

Yael doesn't have an answer for me. But she does put her hand in front of her, palm up and I place mine in hers, which she clasps tight. And then Yael rests her head on my shoulder and we sit there, quietly, high up in our childhood hideaway.

TWENTY-ONE

The next day, Ryan Longford is in town to say goodbye to Lottie.

Maybe once upon a time this would have been an event to keep from the prying eyes of media and paparazzi, but Mr Longford is 80 now. He had a pretty solid career for a time after *Hazards I* and *II* but then in the '90s and early-00s he was better known in Australia as a gameshow host. He doesn't quite inspire the media furore he used to so it's easy enough for him to slip into the hospital all but unnoticed.

Lottie looks worse than ever. Yael and I both came to the hospital very early, and it's her reaction to seeing Lottie that shakes me . . . makes me realise that for a time, we'd all convinced ourselves that she was just sleeping and maybe, despite the doctor's warnings, she could still wake up at any moment. But all of a sudden, her face has become sunken, she sleeps with her mouth wide open and her lips crack easily. Her arms and hands look bonier too, and you can see her purple veins like spider's legs as her skin becomes more translucent.

'Oh *Bubbe*,' Yael whispers, carefully smoothing her fingers against Lottie's forehead after kissing her there, as I choke back tears.

And then Ryan Longford knocks on the door, surprising us both.

Now *The Philadelphia Story* is playing on the TV: easily one of the best Katharine Hepburn movies. She and James Stewart really get to show off their comedic timing playing ex-husband and wife. It's at the scene where Katharine is leaning into him, speaking in this kind of ridiculous Transatlantic accent, as she calls him a snob and tells him, 'The time to make up your mind about people is never.'

'Your grandmother used to get compared to Hepburn a lot,' Mr Longford says, pulling our attention away from the TV.

'Oh yeah?' Yael asks, politely.

He nods. 'Yeah, and it used to really piss her off.'

'Seems like a flattering comparison to me!'

'Nah, she always said male stars get called revelations, heralded as game-changers. But women always get compared to other women, which keeps them in boxes and the same prototypes running around.'

I'm nodding along, because I can kind of see where she was coming from.

'Plus she always had that family legacy looming over her head so I think she was always annoyed when people never judged her in her own right.'

And I know exactly what that's like. Yael must be thinking the same thing, from the look she quickly cuts my way.

Mum swaps with us as the hospital – a friendly changeover between her and Yael, slightly frostier with me – and when we get back to the house we find Jasper and Seth sitting together on the couch, hunched over a mobile phone in the front room.

Yael starts to ask what they're doing, but her dad shushes her and then we hear Kaleb's voice coming through the speaker-phone.

'I will *not* give that woman another *minute* of my time!' my former grandfather bellows.

'Dad, you do know that's also our mother you're talking about?' Seth sighs, removing a pair of reading glasses to rub tiredly at his eyes. 'Our *dying* mother, I might add.'

'Viper of a woman she is too.' Kaleb practically spits the words down the line. 'Why should I be the bigger man, just because she beat me to the grave?'

Yael cautiously approaches her father, and lays a gentle hand on his shoulder which he reaches up for and squeezes. Things have been a little chilled between them too, what with Yael taking time off from uni. But in this moment she has a lot in common with her dad, given they're both children of divorce – even if neither Jasper nor Aunt Constance are anywhere near this level of animosity that Kaleb still holds for Lottie.

A few more choice words and Kaleb hangs up abruptly, leaving his sons looking bone-weary. What pulls them out of their deflation is Yael's suggestion of a good, long Saturday hike along the Cascades Track in South Hobart. And I think Jasper is especially grateful to take her up on the offer, a further olive-branch between them.

So Yael and the uncles head upstairs to get ready for their hike, which leaves me and Poe in the kitchen, and while he's cooking scrambled eggs on toast for late breakfast, I ask him a question.

'Do you think I could invite someone over?'

Poe looks at me over his shoulder. 'Like a friend?'

He's right to be a little shocked, given my scholastic history in Hobart. Once he places the plate in front of me, I add a little sea salt on top while I wait for him to consider.

'Have you told them what's been happening around here, with your grandmother in hospital?'

'Not exactly.'

And then I explain. All about how me and Riya met because of Lottie, in a weird roundabout way, and about Fright Night for Final Girls and Yael telling me to go along and pretty much everything. Except for the thing that is the first Poe asks me about directly.

'And do you like this girl?'

My blush is enough to make him smile and raise his eyebrows at me, suggestively. 'Well, okay then.'

'You don't think it's weird, with everything that's going on – and the way we met?'

Poe shrugs. 'I think Lottie would have been the first to tell you that sometimes relationships have spectacularly bad timing – but that doesn't necessarily mean they're wrong.'

'Whoa, nobody mentioned anything about "relationship".'

Poe nods. 'Fair enough – and yes, I think it would be okay for you to invite her over. But I'd also really appreciate it if you could see fit to telling your mum all this too, okay?'

I give him a look, and he raises his hands in surrender – backing off the topic. But then he adds, 'Ellie, just let me ask you – do you trust this girl?'

I don't even need to think about it anymore. 'Yes.'

'Then I think you may want to tell her what you're going through. Your timing is bound to be off if one of you is kept in the dark.'

TWENTY-TWO

I texted Riya at 10 a.m. and she said she'd be here by 11.

But it's just gone 11.10 a.m. and I'm getting nervous, standing by the wrought-iron gates and looking down Cromwell Street, keeping my eyes peeled.

At 11.13 a.m. I see a figure on a bicycle pumping up Napoleon Street to my right, and I'm a little surprised to look closer and see that it's Riya.

She brakes right in front of me and unclips and removes her helmet. She instantly starts fluffing up her admittedly flattened hair as she breathes deeply. She's wearing a bright yellow Fjällräven Kånken backpack, loose-fitting faded jeans, Converse high-tops and a soft-looking t-shirt with drawings of mermaids all over, in all colours of the rainbow. And there's a fine sheen of sweat collected on her upper lip.

She lets out a huff and says, 'Hi, sorry I'm late – that hill was a killer!'

'You rode here?' I ask, surprised.

Riya looks down at the bike she's sitting on, her legs stretched out either side in stationary position, and smiles. 'Uh, yeah – you inspired me with all your walking around.'

It's then that I hear the familiar sound of the air brakes, and when I turn, I spy the tops of tourist heads sitting on the double-decker as it slowly starts ascending our hill.

I grab Riya's wrist and tug gently. 'Come on, quickly!'

I'm thankful when she doesn't ask questions, but rather hops off her bike and wheels it, following me to the wrought-iron gates that I hold open and usher her through.

'What –' she starts to ask.

But then I'm kick-standing her bike and dragging her behind the high-brick wall to the side. I gently push her back against the wall of climbing purple bougainvillea, her backpack still on her shoulders cushioning her. I hover my hand in front of her mouth to communicate quiet.

Then I look off to the side and hear the familiar sound of the megaphone whining, before a guide begins. 'And to your right, you'll see an example of the Victorian Gothic Revival style of the time in Lovinger House – home to the famous Hobart family of thespians . . .'

But then something wet licks my hand and I pull it back, swallowing the little screech in my throat, and find Riya with her tongue poked out, smiling at me. I start to laugh, but then Riya reaches out with her hand to gently rest her thumb and forefinger on my chin, and I freeze.

'Adam Lovinger nabbed the role of Lancelot in the 1939 big-budget Warner Bros. movie *Lancelot of the Lake*, but it wouldn't be until 1959 that he would win an Oscar.'

I stare at her standing with her black hair all out in curly tendrils against the cloud of bougainvillea, gently holding my chin in her hand. Her lips are still smiling but the longer I look into her brown eyes, the more her smile falls until her lips are barely open, and her breathing becomes shallow as she looks at me too.

'Which brings us to Charlotte "Lottie" Lovinger of the famous *Hazards* film franchise. She bashed her way onto the world stage with a cricket bat, in the horror zombie movies shot entirely around Sydney . . .'

I blink at the booming mention of Lottie and shake myself a little. I step back so that Riya's hand has to fall and the moment passes.

'Now, folks, we'll continue our run through historic Battery Point of Old Hobart Town.' Then I hear the sound of the bus pulling away.

'Does that happen often?' Riya asks me.

'Every three hours.'

'Wow, that's intense.'

'It's not so bad, so long as you avoid the front gate. We can't hear them from the house, and they can't see much except the top of our roof.' As I talk, I turn around and start to walk. I feel Riya going for her bike to push it and follow me. I notice we keep a little distance between us as we amble up the driveway.

It's not until we get to right in front of the house that Riya lets out a low whistle and I turn to see her with her head back and neck craning to take it all in.

'You can leave your bike here,' I say, waving to just beside the doorway. And Riya does just that, and then she joins me at the little entryway to our medieval front door. She pauses at the doorpost and points to the covered *mezuzah* that's tilted and nailed there.

'What's this?'

I explain about the wooden plate cover, with parchment inside and the words of God inscribed. *Mezuzah* literally means 'doorpost' and some Orthodox people take that to dictate that one should hang at the doorway of every room in a house but we have just this one, at the entrance.

'Is it to ward off evil spirits, or something?'

'It's more like a kind of rule to have one, or a blessing on the house.'

'Ah, for us it's mango leaves and marigold,' Riya says, and we share a smile.

And then I'm pushing the big wooden door open, and Riya stops talking as she steps inside, and then turns in a slow circle on the spot with wide eyes darting all around.

'Whoa.'

It's a lot, I know.

There's a sitting room to one side, a long hallway leading down to the kitchen, a grand staircase, high ceilings, portrait and landscape paintings of every size up and down the hallway walls and then all the quirky little details like tiger-paws for coat racks and the tall grandfather clock beneath the stairs.

'This is amazing.'

I don't say anything. Instead I gesture for Riya to sit at the little wooden bench underneath the coat rack.

'So I've been meaning to ask, exactly how Jewish *are* you?'

And I laugh as we both pull our shoes off to line them up in the shoe rack.

'Ummmm . . .'

'Sorry, oh wow – that came out horribly! It's like when people ask where I'm from, and I'm like, "Dude, I had ancestors here during the Gold Rush!"'

'No, no – it's okay. Harvey, my grandfather, was Lottie's only secular husband, and my dad is secular too. I guess that makes me . . . a quarter Jewish? Or something? We celebrate Hanukkah, not Christmas – but for instance, Yom Kippur was this week and we didn't do anything. Sometimes we will, but this year with Lottie and everything – there was just too much going on.'

At this Riya takes a deep breath and frowns. 'Am I over-stepping anything if I ask how your grandmother is doing after surgery?' I must take a beat too long to think what to say to that, because Riya hurriedly adds, 'I'm not asking for the film club or, like, in a fangirl capacity – I promise! Just, as a friend.'

That word again – *friend.* And Riya asking after Lottie because she still thinks she's just recovering from surgery . . . I'm saved from answering one, and from agonising over the other, by the sound of Poe calling out via the wind-tunnel of the hallway that leads to the kitchen.

'Hello the house!' he yells, and I roll my eyes.

Mentally I tell myself I will have to explain to her eventually about Lottie. But I'm also thankful that Poe just saved me, and I'm able to gently elbow Riya and say, 'Come on, meet one of my grandfathers.'

Poe is standing casually by the island in our rustic, open-plan kitchen. He's randomly holding a tea towel with a May Gibbs gumnut babies print, and I wonder if he didn't pick it up as a prop. He's wearing dark blue slacks, and a light blue v-neck jumper and honestly looks like he could be in a menswear catalogue. When he sees Riya and me, his smile is warm and genuine and I feel a radiant burst of pure love for him.

'You must be Riya!' he says, and then he holds out his hand and she walks to meet him.

Riya's eyes are wide and her mouth slightly open as she says, 'You're Poe Tuhana!'

'I am.'

She pumps his hand twice and then they let go, and she manages to snap her mouth shut to smile at him. 'I'm a really big fan! Your costume work on *The Captain,* and *Seven Hills* – oh, and the regency romance *Something Like Love*, oh my gosh!'

I feel like she could go on, but then Poe says thank you so demurely and with a little head-bow that she gets a dreamy look in her eye for a moment and I'm able to jump back in.

'I'm going to show Riya around, okay?'

Poe nods and then pulls out one of the bench seats at the island, which is when I notice a bunch of cookbooks spread out.

'I'm just going to be here, in the kitchen, deciding on what meals to cook for this week.'

'Okay.'

'I'll be right here if you need me.'

And then I'm hustling Riya out the door and spinning around once she's out of range to give Poe the *thumbs up* sign and to congratulate him on being *very smooth* – to which he infuriatingly just gives me a little *salute* in return.

TWENTY-THREE

We end the tour in Lottie's room of all places.

We'd been around the grounds and to all the communal rooms – I'd even shown Riya the widow's roof walk. But then we'd come to the blue room, my room, and I'd clammed up. In a bid to deflect from the heat climbing up my neck and cheeks, I'd side-stepped to the other side of the hallway and walked down to Lottie's door, taken a deep breath, and then reached for the brass handle and pushed.

From the entrance Riya admires the large four-poster bed and big bay window looking out onto the garden.

I'm the one who steps gingerly inside, and she follows me – instantly drawn to the picture frames on the round-mirrored dresser, while I take a moment to inhale the familiar scent of Lottie's freesia perfume that still lingers faintly.

There's a headshot of Harvey, looking handsome and brooding, and one of Lottie and Poe on their wedding day. Baby photos of my mum and the uncles, and then a whole-family one (minus the grandfathers Kaleb and Shane) taken when Poe was at the top of the stairs, looking down to photograph us. I would have been about nine, in that one.

'Does your mum remember him?' Riya asks, and I follow her eyes to the small frame of Harvey.

'Not really. She once told me that the way she thinks of him is in terms of his movies, and the characters he played.'

'Oh wow, that's kind of sad?'

'Yeah. He was only twenty-seven when he died, and my mum was just a kid. So, the way she got to know and remember him was from those handful of films he did.'

'That's tough.'

'It's better than nothing, though.'

Riya moves to the bay window, where you can see the big yellow wattle tree down below. I took her there just before, to show her the bronzed Tasmanian tiger.

'Can I ask, how did he die again?'

I walk across the room, and we both sit down at the bench seat in front of the window.

'He got drunk one night and wrapped his car around a tree, in Sydney.'

'Oh my God, I'm so sorry – that's awful.'

'Yeah. Lottie never really talks about him, and my mum once told me that the memories she does have of him are of his being kind of sad and distant, but that could also just be the characters he tended to play. So – who knows?'

'Have you ever seen his movies?'

I nod once. 'Yeah – *The Harp in the South.* We even had to study it last year in English.'

'No!' Riya looks a little shocked, and I laugh. 'That must be so weird for you; other people's set-text and classic filmography is like your family's home movies . . .'

I shrug. 'His character is so angry and hurt in that film too. It made me sad to think that he was almost stuck in that role, acting it out over and over again even after he passed away, and that's how my mum got to know him. And then to have a bunch of senior school students pick him apart in essays and quiz questions too.'

'When you put it like that, it does sound freaky,' Riya says. 'Like he's trapped in time and the movie.'

And I feel a little shiver race down my spine to realise that's how I feel too. About my own role in *Blood & Jacaranda* – it's my constant trap playing on a loop and for everyone to see.

We're quiet for a bit, and then Riya says, 'Your house is really beautiful, Ellie.'

'Well, it's not really mine. It belongs to all the family – it's just that Lottie is the one who is here permanently. Mum, Dad and I lived here with her when I was growing up, and until we moved to London – for my mum and dad's work.'

It's a half-lie, and one I'm glad Riya doesn't pick apart beyond asking, 'I know your dad's a theatre director, but what does your mum do?'

'Kind of, *everything*?' Riya laughs at that. 'She studied law and commerce, went in a totally different direction to Lottie, maybe a bit rebelliously – and then she met my dad while studying in Melbourne, and found herself in another version of a theatrical family, without really meaning to. Now she runs the business side, because my dad does not have a brain for that. She handles his contracts, deals with the lawyers, and insurance companies, the investors, grant applications – all that stuff that actually makes a creative thing come together, she does.'

'That's cool.'

'I think so. And lately my dad's been encouraging her to branch out – link up with an arts foundation she really cares about and help them run things.'

'Do you think she will?'

I shrug. 'I hope so – she's really good at helping fund an artistic vision.'

Riya nods, but then she says, 'Well, it must be easy when you come from money and have a legacy.'

'What?'

And she shrugs. 'All this? It's amazing. But it's not ordinary.'

'No, I know that.' I frown.

She shakes her head and winces. 'Sorry, this is coming out bitter and I don't mean for that. It's just . . . I have to work my butt off at the cinema just to get by, and even if I happen to get into AFTRS when it's already really competitive, I'll have to have saved enough money to make my way doing a degree that nobody in my family really understands or believes in.'

'They don't want you studying music composition?'

Riya scoffs. 'Ah, *no* – they'd prefer I study pharmacy, or engineering like my brother Faris is. They'll be happy for me if I get in, but they can't help me out when I'm in Sydney – and they know I'm not exactly choosing an area that pays big money or has a lot of job security or even many opportunities.'

When I don't say anything, Riya adds, 'I just wish I had something like your legacy to fall back on, you know? With a family who totally understands a desire to pursue a career in the Arts and could open doors for me, and a little cushioning to help out while I'm studying would be nice too. Studying and pursuing a career in the Arts, it . . . well, it tends to be a luxury only a few people can afford – and only certain types of people.'

There are echoes here of my conversation with Yael the other day and the idea of a 'legacy' I'm upholding – but I'm embarrassed to admit that it never occurred to me to look at my life in quite this way. 'I've never thought of it like that,' I say.

She sighs. 'I'm in a weird mood – ignore me. I've got my piano exam coming up, and my car just bombed out on me. That's the real reason I rode my bike here, actually. And all of this,' she waves her hands in the air, indicating the house, 'it's just a lot for one Saturday afternoon.'

I grasp onto the one thing she said that I might be able to help out with. 'Piano exam?'

Riya nods. 'Yeah, and it's seriously messing with my head. I can only practise at school, or on my old secondhand keyboard at home and it's just not the same . . .'

I hold a finger up. 'Come with me.'

We go back downstairs. In the kitchen we pass Poe, who smiles at us as we run past and out through the back door to the sunroom, where we keep the white baby grand piano.

'Oh my . . . *Wow*!' is all Riya can say.

I was avoiding showing her this side of the house because Poe is right through the connecting hallway, and now that she's here and her eyes bugging out, I'm also self-conscious that she'll think I'm showing off or something. But I push that thought aside and gesture for her to take a seat, which she does.

'So? Play something.'

And then she does. A few keys are out of tune, but under Riya's surprisingly nimble fingers, running up and down the keys, you can hardly notice. She plays something I don't recognise, but it's light and beautiful and I'm amazed at how much personality Riya is imbuing in the piece.

It's so good that Poe claps loud and long when she's finished, and we both turn around to see him leaning in the doorway.

'Pardon my interruption,' he says, 'But was that Fanny Mendelssohn?'

'It was – *Piano sonata in C minor*.'

And then Poe exaggeratedly grabs at his chest, as though to clutch his heart, before bowing out and leaving us alone again.

'That felt really good, and it was just what I needed – thank you.'

I come to sit beside Riya on the piano bench. 'You're right, of course – about the whole luxury to pursue the Arts thing. It's a privilege, for sure. Just because I was born into it and didn't ask for it, doesn't mean I don't benefit from it – every day.'

Riya shakes her head, but I hold up a hand and she stops. 'It's something I'll work on remembering and being more conscious of – if you also promise to take advantage of any help *I* can offer.' I smile and nod at the piano. 'Because you are *amazing*. And any time you want to come over to practise, just know that you can.'

And because she's smiling again, and I don't know how to talk about Lottie now without ruining this moment, I say, 'Play it once, Sam, for old time's sake.'

TWENTY-FOUR

Yael insists that I drive us to Fright Night on Sunday, in Harvey's EH wagon.

I'm already not the most confident of drivers but adding in the wideness of the vintage car and pencil-thin wheel, plus no reverse camera monitors and I'm sweating so much the whole time that I can hardly hold the wheel. Yael makes a big show of pointing out the mothers pushing prams who are outpacing us as I gingerly take roundabouts and corners at a snail's pace. But I make it and right on time, even if I have to park about five kilometres away for just the right spot to sail into, with no reversing or judging the width required. Yael side-eyes me the whole time.

The box office is busy, and Riya waves at us to go downstairs while she finishes up her shift and the queue that's ten-people deep.

When we get down there, Jen is setting up and waves at us, then comes over and I introduce her to Yael. I can't even begin to guess what the Auslan sign for 'cousin' may be, but after attending the first film club I did Google the Auslan alphabet out of curiosity so I think to make a small letter 'c' with my right hand, which has Yael raising an eyebrow at me.

'She might think you're calling me something else . . .' she says, and I blush.

Jen watches our lips closely and breaks out in a big grin, then with one of her hands she lifts the 'c' I made and moves it from one corner of my mouth to the other.

Yael mimics the movement herself, and Jen gives two thumbs up in approval.

Then I keep the conversation going by saying, 'They're really busy tonight.' I hope that she can understand me.

She does – because then she poses like she's Superman, with one fist out to her side, and the other shooting straight up in the air and I guess at what she means.

Yael doesn't guess. Instead she whips out her phone and types in the notes app, reading aloud as she does before showing Jen the text she's written: 'There's a superhero movie out?'

Jen nods, and then rolls her eyes.

I'm also momentarily embarrassed that Yael just highlighted a really obvious way for me to communicate with Jen that I hadn't yet tried, but before I can blush fully there comes a yell from the back of the room.

'Hey, don't diss comic-book movies!'

I spin around to find Kate and Maria wandering in. One of them – Maria – signs what Kate just said and Jen replies just as quick.

'Jen says she'll respect comic-book movies as soon as studios employ more than one female director at a time,' Maria says, and then she nods as though to say – fair point.

'How about – as soon as they cast Disabled actors and directors to tell stories of Disability in comic-book adaptations?' Riya says as she sails in, and then she taps Jen on the shoulder to repeat what she just said in sign, and Jen replies by holding her hands out flat and shaking them in praise.

Jen and Riya make introductions between the girls and Yael, who makes fast friends among them when she points to the *Buffy the Vampire Slayer* t-shirt that Maria is wearing and they launch into a deep discussion about the almost entirely silent episode, *Hush* from season four – apparently.

When Riya sees my blank look at all the *Buffy* talk, she turns to me. Tonight her collar-tips are tiger faces, smiling at me with all their teeth.

'Did you know there is a whole sub-genre of Deaf horror cinema?' she says, signing at the same time.

'Really? That's so cool!'

'Oh, you haven't lived until you've seen 1975 American horror classic, *Deafula*.'

'As in . . . ?'

'*Dracula*, but entirely in American Sign Language – yes!' Riya smiles wide.

I turn to Jen and ask if she liked it, to which she grimaces in reply.

'Oh no, really?'

Jen starts signing and Riya says, 'What? It's a schlocky '70s horror film made on a tiny budget. I'm a way bigger fan of *A Quiet Place*.'

This time it's my turn to grimace when I admit I haven't seen it, and all Riya can do is roll her eyes while Jen feigns shock-horror and throws her hands up at me, before looking between me and Riya as though to say: *fix this error.*

So I hold my hands up in defeat. 'I'll add it to the list.'

'You better, or Jen will never stop nagging you,' Riya says.

And then everyone is settling in once again, to their same seats as last time, while Jen and Riya move to the front of the room and begin. I take a moment to look behind me and wave for Yael to come join me on the two-seater, but she makes a show of shaking her head and grinning, choosing instead to sit with Maria and the girls at the back.

Riya launches in after the acknowledgement of country. '*Tigers Are Not Afraid* – or *Vuelven* in the original Spanish – is the 2017 Mexican crime fantasy film, written and directed by Issa López.' Riya finger-spells the word *Vuelven* which she says she thinks means 'to return'.

Jen takes over. 'The film follows five children orphaned by a drug war unfolding in an unnamed Mexican city, as they band together to escape the cartels and ghosts being created every day by gun violence and power struggles. There's also a particular focus on the women and children who are – as in reality – the most unfairly targeted and harmed by this ongoing systemic violence.'

Then Riya says, 'Without further ado, we give you – *Tigers Are Not Afraid* for the second October FNFG film-club screening.'

•

The movie is amazing. Maybe not perfect, and not as scary as it could have been but I'm surprised to find that I'm crying when Riya brings the lights up and smiles at me especially. When I turn around to see if Yael was just as affected, I blush to realise she's been watching me and Riya intently and she gives me a knowing smile, before I have to whip back around to avoid her seeing my reddening cheeks.

Ah-Pei begins the discussion in the restaurant after. 'I loved it, and it reminded me of Guillermo del Toro's *The Devil's Backbone*.'

'Why, because they're both Mexican directors?' Kate asks, and Ah-Pei narrows her eyes at her.

'No, because of that thing del Toro once said.' Ah-Pei looks to Riya and Jen for help. 'How American horror stories focus on the destruction of the body, but Spanish and Latin-American horror is all about the soul?'

'Okay, whoa,' says Kate.

'See, I told you so!' says Ah-Pei. 'I think that's why I prefer them too – they remind me of the ghost-stories my *nenek* tells us kids. There's always a lesson in them.'

'You can definitely see that difference by comparing *Tigers* to *Slumber Party Massacre*,' I say, and then I go a little red, until Riya claps excitedly, before clarifying.

'Well, technically you can't compare them because *Slumber Party* is a serial-killer slasher, and *Tigers* is a ghost story – totally different sub-genres, but you're getting it!'

Jen raps her hands on the table to get Kate's attention, and then signs for Kate to interpret. 'Twenty per cent less nerdiness, dude.'

'Okay, okay,' Riya laughs, 'but it is fascinating how American horror differs from . . .'

The talk goes on, and I'm happy to sit back and let their aforementioned nerdiness wash over me . . . but then I realise that's too simple, and their appreciation goes deeper. There's love and admiration mixed into their discussion – and the more they say, the more I realise how they're constantly connecting aspects of the film and its genre back to their real lives.

At one point, Yael catches my eye and rolls hers, but she looks content and fascinated by the discussion too. I wonder if we both realise how different it is on this side, loving something because it speaks to you, not because it's tied to your family history and legacy.

'Can you imagine Lottie here, listening to all this?' Yael leans over to whisper to me, and – I can, weirdly. I think Lottie would have loved this tangible proof of how movies – art, really – changes people's lives. How it comes to mean more to them than a couple of distracted hours at the cinema. Lets them know themselves deeper.

Eventually the talk shifts to the next films on the roster, and Halloween fast-approaching.

'And we have no plans for a new membership drive, so we're screwed,' says Maria.

I blink at the change in tone and topic, feel the FNFG members shift uncomfortably, before Yael asks the question for me. 'What membership drive?'

Jen taps Riya on the shoulder, and when she starts signing Riya interprets. 'It's fine. We just had this big event planned around Lottie Lovinger doing this ticketed Q&A for us so we could raise some money and get more members to maybe sign up . . .'

'Raise money for what?' I ask.

Riya and Jen share a look, and then Jen nods a go-ahead for Riya to answer. 'Once Jen and I graduate and go off to uni, FNFG will be in the girls' hands.' She gestures at Kate, Maria and Ah-Pei.

'We really wanted to help them get more people to join so the club could go on, keep growing and expanding – and one way we thought to do that was to make it as inclusive and accessible as possible.'

Jen raps her fist on the table, to get Riya's attention and then starts signing. 'We had an idea to buy new TitleCraps,' here Riya blushes and adds, 'Title*Caps* technology – but they're really expensive, so we wanted to help the cinema out in purchasing them ourselves.'

I turn and briefly explain this colloquialism to Yael, who says to Riya and Jen, 'Okay, two birds with one stone, you get Lottie to do an event to both help raise money, and as a membership drive?'

Jen waits for Riya to stop signing, and then Jen looks to me and Yael to nod, exactly.

'To be fair, we've wanted to get Lottie Lovinger to come and do a Q&A with us for the *longest* time,' Maria says. 'I mean, a scream-queen legend like her, living right here in Hobart – never fails to amaze me!'

The others all nod in agreement at this sentiment, before Kate adds, 'We tried all different ways of contacting her, even going through her agents and then addressing letters to her house, since we all know about *that* place. But she never replied or got back to us.'

Yael leans forward, frowning and looking between Jen and Riya. 'But she agreed in the end, right? So how did you change her mind?' Yael asks seriously.

It's Riya who explains this time, and Ah-Pei who whips her phone out to type messages to Jen as Riya speaks. 'We don't really know,' Riya says. 'We wrote to her back in July, except this time we explained our situation – that two of our five members would soon be leaving us, and we wanted to boost membership and raise money to make screenings more accessible, and maybe she'd consider doing an event and speaking publicly about *Blood & Jacaranda* for the first time in years to drum up interest, and . . .'

'She agreed,' Kate says.

Yael turns her head sharply to look at me, and I have to avert my eyes. I feel my heartbeat quicken and my neck start to creep with red as I begin to wonder if my and Lottie's meeting in Melbourne in late June had anything to do with her change of heart? Or is it all just coincidence, and I'm still trying to cling to some sort of redemption story for Lottie, when it comes to me?

'She actually offered to buy the program for us outright,' Riya says. 'But we thought it'd mean more if people got a sense of community out of the event, and investing in the film club. So instead, she said she'd cover any outstanding costs not made up by ticket sales.'

'Wait,' I say. 'This sounds like you actually spoke to her?'

Riya nods. 'I did – she gave us her private phone number in the letter she sent, and told us to call her, and so I did and she was –' Riya smiles at the memory. 'It was kind of surreal. She sounded exactly like she does in the movies, you know?' Then she rolls her eyes at me, as though to say *Well of course you know!* 'But she really did have that Lovinger, I don't know . . .'

'Lilt,' I provide, and Riya's eyes light up.

'Yes! Lilt is exactly it!'

'And when did you last speak to her?' My heart is beating fast as I await her answer.

'When I was letting her know that we'd sent the flyers off to the printer, and I'd pop one in the mail for her – so it would have been the day before our September film club, on the twenty-second. I remember because she'd asked what our pick was for that Sunday, and it was Jordan Peele's *Us*. She said he was one of the most exciting writers and directors working right now, and I asked if we could put that in our Q&A. Find out who else she has her eye on.'

And my heart clenches to realise that that was the day before her stroke.

'Hey – maybe we can still get Ms Lovinger to help us with a membership drive? If she'd let us take a video of her promoting us that we could share to the State Cinema website or something?' Ah-Pei asks.

Maria rolls her eyes. 'Facial lymph-nodes surgery is surgery of the throat, genius.'

Ah-Pei snaps her fingers. 'Well, what if we taught her to sign a message? Hello?' She points to Riya, who is signing for Jen as Ah-Pei speaks. 'We're all learning, so maybe she can too? If we give her a message to memorise?'

Then everything goes quiet, and I realise they're all looking at me and Yael.

I swallow and wipe my sweating hands on my jeans. 'I . . . I don't think she's able to. I'm so sorry. I can ask, but – I just don't think it's possible.'

Riya reaches over and stills one of my hands that I'm currently wiping repeatedly on my jeans. 'It's okay, Ellie – we understand.'

I also notice Yael noticing Riya's hands covering mine, so I'm almost relieved when Ah-Pei chimes in with, 'Well – what about you?' Even as Riya grimaces.

Kate also thinks it's a good idea. 'Yeah, the Halloween screening is *Blood & Jacaranda* after all – and you've never spoken about it publicly. That could get even more attention than Lottie would have!'

I'm shaking my head already.

'It's one of the definitive horror movies of our generation too,' says Maria. 'You'd appeal more to younger members, potentially, and that's exactly what we need to keep Final Girls going for longer!'

'My dad could help us promote it,' Ah-Pei jumps back in. 'If we give enough time, he could run a feature about it in the *Hobart Town Gazette*!'

'She can't,' Yael tries for me.

'Well, why not?'

It's Riya who saves me. She makes a chopping motion with her hands, and everyone goes silent.

'Ellie and Lottie are not participating, and that's final. We just have to get over it and find another way to get new members.'

Even Jen looks a little despondent, and my heart squeezes in guilt.

'Hey! It's only October the thirteenth. We know Halloween celebrations are getting bigger and bigger every year. Our film club is the perfect way to spend the evening leading up to All Saints' Eve. I really do think we can still do this and get a boost.'

Once she says that, everyone deflates slightly, before agreeing to wrap it up and go home, which is when I offer to drive Riya.

'You? Drove here? You?'

Yael snickers at this, but nods in confirmation.

'Well, I know you said your car has conked out . . .' I say.

'It has, and I've been relying on lifts to and from school with Arin, who drives like our dādī. So – thank you!'

'Oh, Ellie doesn't drive any better – trust me!' Yael laughs, and Riya smiles.

When Riya signs to Jen that she's catching a ride home with me and Yael, Jen raises her eyebrows and possibly even wiggles them a little. Riya replies with a gentle swat to her arm before she and I stand up. But then I turn to see Yael hasn't budged and I ask her if she's ready.

'Oh, I'm not going home yet,' she says, and pops another spoonful of mint-choc chip into her mouth, before adding, 'I'm catching up with some friends tonight. I've got a car on the way.'

I frown down at her, but Yael looks so calm and collected and even a little – I want to say – smug? She waves the fingers of one hand at me and says, 'I'll text you when I get there and when I'm on my way home. You and Riya have a good drive now.'

And there's really nothing else I can say, so I step away with Riya and we head downstairs so she can collect her things from the staff locker room. When she's got her purple raincoat on against the cold Hobart night, we step outside the State Cinema and I pretend to do lunges on the spot.

'Um – what is this?' Riya asks.

I pull my right leg up behind me and hold my ankle – a little hard to do in jeans, but I manage. 'Oh, just warming up for the hike,' I say.

'The hike?'

'To my car,' I say. Then I start walking and wave my hand behind me. 'Come on – we want to beat the dawn!'

TWENTY-FIVE

Realistically, it's only us crossing the street to get to Harvey's old electric-blue wagon and it's still the sole car in the parking lot behind the post office.

Riya pretends to huff and puff from our walk, but upon seeing the car she lets out a low whistle. 'I wondered who this belonged to at Sami's party that night.'

I shrug a little self-consciously, remembering her words from the other day. 'It was my grandfather's. Heavily remodelled and updated, but still his.' Then I open the driver's side door and get in, as Riya does the same on the passenger side.

She reverently touches the similarly electric-blue dashboard and admires the white leather bench-seating, which means there's no gear-box or handbrake between us like in regular cars.

I'm about to start it up and crank the heating when I look at the sky through the windshield and admire the cascade of stars high above.

'You don't get a sky like that in Melbourne, or London,' I say, and Riya leans forward slightly to admire it too. 'I think it's unique to Hobart.'

'Okay, so maybe we shouldn't waste it?' says Riya.

I've started inching the car forward out of the parking lot when she asks this and quickly look over at her and then back in front as I come out to the parking-lot driveway.

'What do you suggest?' I ask. But before she can think too much about it, I have an idea – a memory from the night of whoever-Sami-is and their party. 'What about Rosny Hill?'

We look to each other and smile, and that's all it takes for me to turn right out of the lot and head towards the Tasman Bridge. Riya offers to take care of the soundtrack for our drive, and selects songs from G Flip to Raja Kumari that play as we start crawling and winding around Rose Bay.

But once I park us in a spot at the Rosny Hill lookout, she stops the music and we don't say anything. We just take it in. Hobart in the distance – lights like stars, and stars blanketing the sky. The second the engine cuts off everything is still and quiet and beautiful. And we admire all the little lights of our town.

All the little lights.

And I remember that scene – the one Corinne told me about, the one I watched for the first time just a few days ago. Hannah-Jane and Marty admiring their town that's lost and overrun by the dead, even though from far away it all looks just the same and beautiful. Everything is changed, but nothing will ever be the same.

'I lied,' I say.

Riya turns to me. 'What?'

'The reason my grandmother can't help you is not because she's recovering from surgery.' I let my grip fall from the steering wheel and look over at Riya looking at me, and I tell her. 'Lottie is dying.'

And then I can't stop talking. 'Stroke. Literally, the day after you spoke to her on the phone. She had a stroke in her kitchen at home. They operated on her brain to alleviate the bleed and pressure but she won't recover. She's on morphine and they call it end-of-life care because that's what it is: a very slow process of dying.'

I shake my head. 'It's also why I'm here – in Hobart – after being gone so long. It's why the whole family is, slowly, coming home. To say goodbye and make sure she's not alone, because you're not supposed to be alone at the end. And I couldn't tell you – we're not supposed to tell *anyone* because Lottie didn't want us to. She wants to die quietly, with just the family, some friends. So that's what we've been trying to do, everything she asked for – in the end.'

I realise I'm crying. I very ungracefully wipe my nose on my long sleeve and gently swipe under my eyes. And in response, Riya slides along the bench seat to be closer to me.

I think she's saying *I'm sorry, I'm so sorry* but I can't be sure because then I'm almost hyperventilating from crying so hard. It's the first time I've let myself go, thinking about Lottie and all those years of silence and the last few months of bad blood; that I'll never get another chance to yell at her, or tell her, or forgive her, or ask her *why why why* and it suddenly feels bitterly unfair. And so, I cry.

And then Riya is holding me as I shake from the tears, and I drop my head to her shoulder and reach my arms underneath hers to wrap around her middle, the way she's reached around to hold me and squeeze me to her.

Until eventually, I swear we're breathing at the same exact time. Our hearts feeling like they're beating in sync too because I can feel hers there, pressing right against my chest.

We pull apart so we can look at each other.

'Ellie,' she breathes my name, 'Ellie.'

And then I'm kissing her.

Or she's kissing me.

Cupping my face so gently in her hands, our lips meet softly and then a little harder as our breathing gets heavier. I may even bite her bottom lip a little, until she opens to me and our kiss deepens and one of her hands goes to the back of my head, cradles me and pushes us closer together, while my hands find her waist and try to pull her even closer to me.

We kiss and breathe and beat together.

And then we come down, slowly. Our breathing evening out, heartbeats ticking slower before they explode, and bit by bit we draw apart.

But she's still holding my face so gently in her hands, so that when I take a deep breath and close my eyes, she kisses me there too – atop each eyelid, as she says my name again and again before letting me go.

When I open my eyes, she's looking at me with such sympathy, but there's heat there too and I'm glad – even more so when she says, 'I've wanted to do that for the longest time.'

I kiss her quick and hard, because I have to after she says that, even resting my hand at her collarbone, burrowing in a little beneath the collar of her work shirt to feel the heat of her skin there, while her tiger tips seem to smile devilishly at me.

When we pull apart this time, we keep our foreheads pressed together for a moment as I speak softly. 'I wanted you, and I wanted to tell you – but I couldn't.'

'It's okay, Ellie – I understand. And I'm *so sorry.*'

And before I've even thought to ask, Riya adds, 'I won't tell anybody, I promise.'

'I know. I trust you.'

Because I do. I trust her, and I want her – again. There's so much we still need to talk about, but right now it's enough that when I reach for her, she comes to me, and our lips meet again and again and again.

TWENTY-SIX

The first person I tell is Yael. The following morning I wake her up the same unceremonious way she once did me – by sneaking into the rose room and holding her nose for a second until she flails awake.

And before she can even work up the strength to frown at me, I declare, 'I kissed Riya. Several times.'

She heaves herself to a sitting position, adjusts the silk scarf that keeps her pile of black curls in a protected pineapple atop her head, and then pats the spot next to her for me to come sit.

'Take it from the top, from the moment you said goodbye to all of us last night.'

'Seriously?'

'Yes!' she all but screeches. 'Paint the scene for me, build suspense – reveal character, *tell me*!'

And so, I do. We lounge on her bed in the rose room, both of us staring up at the plaster rose on the ceiling, and I tell Yael absolutely everything. By the end she's up on one elbow looking down at me wide-eyed and smiling, and I think she's weirdly proud of me.

'I've never seen you like this,' Yael finally says, and I raise an eyebrow for her to continue. 'You are frustratingly scarce on social media, and we kinda skipped the staying-up-late and giggling about our crushes portion of growing up together. So I'm not sure if you've felt this way before . . . ?'

Yael is looking at me expectantly, and I understand there's a question she's not directly asking in there too. I look into her eyes to answer. 'Let's just say that while watching *Cat on a Hot Tin Roof* one day, I came to the realisation that I didn't have to choose, and I could fantasise about *both* Paul Newman and Elizabeth Taylor and that felt very right for me,' Here I raise my eyebrows comically.

Yael lets out a burst of laughter and cups her hands to her face, then smirks. 'For me it's classic Cary Grant or Harry Belafonte though, in case *you* were curious.'

I laugh, then go on. 'There's been a couple of girls in the past, one guy once upon a time, but it's never been serious or gone very far . . . and I've never felt about anyone the way I do about Riya.'

Yael nods, and then asks, 'And so, what does Aunt Louise think of all this?'

I scoot down lower on the bed beside Yael, who pushes herself down too so we each have our heads lying flat on the pillows.

'She and Dad know, and are really great . . .' I say.

'None of that "it's just a phase" crap then?'

I scrunch up my nose. 'No, thankfully.' And then I pause. 'But since I haven't spoken to Mum in days, she doesn't yet know that Riya even exists.'

Yael lets out a long sigh, and then very gently reprimands me. 'Ellie!'

I wince, but don't say anything. Yael knows – the whole house does! – that Mum and I are not speaking, and thanks to our rooftop talk the other day, Yael knows why too.

We're quiet for a bit, and then Yael clears her throat. 'I'll just say that you and your mum have enough on your plate to sort through, without keeping this from her too.'

I don't reply. I don't need to. Yael understands, and then I feel her shoulder shrug against mine as she quietly says, 'I am happy for you, and I'm really glad you told me, though.'

And I realise by the lightness in my chest that I am too.

TWENTY-SEVEN

Later Yael has left for another shift sitting vigil at the hospital and I'm sitting on the edge of my bed, about to wander downstairs for my breakfast when my phone suddenly starts vibrating, and then rings in my hand. I smile and answer before the second ring can start when I see who it is.

'It's you.'

'It's me,' Riya says.

And I think we must both be smiling goofily into space because we don't speak for a second, and then Riya gives a nervous little laugh. 'So, my piano recital is this week.'

'Oh yeah?'

'Yeah, and I was wondering if I could maybe come over for one more practice session?'

'Practising. Piano.'

'Yes. Right now, actually – I've got a free study period.'

I'm already standing up and heading for the stairs, one hand on the balustrade as I say, 'I'll come pick you up . . .'

'Actually.'

I stop, paused in front of one of the many portrait paintings of a Lovinger descendant – I forget which one – hanging along the wall.

'I'm already here.'

I continue descending and take the last stair in a bounding leap, hastily tell Riya I'm coming down to meet her and yank the front door open. I glance at my watch and see it's 8 a.m. Riya, dressed in her school uniform, is indeed by the gates and holding her bike and smiling as wide as I imagine I must be when she sees me.

I open the gate enough to let her wheel the bike and herself in, then she stands holding it by the handlebars to her side and we face each other – continuing to smile like loons – until I'm finally the first one to speak.

'Nice uniform.'

Riya looks down at herself then back at me, and I'm a little delighted to find she's blushing.

'Yeah, I've only got a couple hours but I really wanted to squeeze in some more practising. On the piano,' after another beat she adds, 'for my recital.'

I nod along with each point, then raise an eyebrow at her.

'And I wanted to see you again after last night,' she says.

She tucks an escaped curl behind her ear. I'm a little sad to find her hair is in a loose plait hanging over her shoulder, and I'm also a little sad to find that she's now looking at me a little uneasily.

'I just wanted to double-check that I didn't cross a line last night. I know you're grieving, or preparing to be grieving and I'm so honoured that you confided in me, but I didn't want you to think I took advantage of you in your . . .'

While she talks, I reach for one of her hands and I pull her gently along with me, so that she has to let the bike fall to the ground.

Then I walk her the couple of steps to the brick wall of purple bougainvillea, turn around and take her by the shoulders, manoeuvring her to stand in front of the wall of flowers again, just as she did the first day she came to Lovinger House. Once she's in position, frowning at me and about to open her mouth no doubt to ask what the heck I'm doing – I lean forward and kiss her.

We got pretty good at this last night, so it doesn't take long for the kiss to deepen – for her to open her mouth fully to me and for my hands to move from her shoulders down to her hips, to press her against me and feel again the way her heart beats against mine.

After a decade or maybe just a couple minutes of this we pull apart, both of us breathing deeply until I regain enough oxygen to say, 'Just so we're clear.'

Riya can only nod her head and look a little dazed. And then we're walking up the driveway together, her wheeling her bike and me bumping her shoulder and both of us constantly turning and smiling at one another.

We sit like this too when she's practising piano, close together as she runs her fingers up and down the keys. She insists she doesn't mind that I'm this close, even as I slide down to give her a little more wingspan.

When she asks who else is home and if she's disturbing anyone, I feel good being able to tell her honestly that two of my uncles are at the hospital with Lottie, while Poe, my mum and my third uncle have gone to the Hobart Synagogue.

'To pray – or worship? Or, I'm sorry I don't know . . .'

I smile and bump her shoulder again to let her know it's okay. 'Actually, the Hobart Jewish community is really small. We don't even have a permanent Rabbi at the synagogue, even though it's Australia's oldest. Services are normally Shabbat mornings and the occasional Friday night, and the building is shared by the Orthodox and Progressive segment that we identify with.' I shake my head. 'But today they've just gone down to meet with some of the members, because they've decided it's time to tell them.'

'I'm so sorry, Ellie. This must all be really hard.'

We're quiet for a bit, and then Riya begins playing again. She plays the same song over and over ahead of her recital. It sounds beautiful and perfect to me every time, but after the fourth turn Riya leans back and stretches, cracks her knuckles and asks for any requests.

I shrug. 'I don't know. What about something like what you want to do in films, composing or whatever.'

'Oh, some horror music?'

'Sure.'

She plays something that doesn't sound all that creepy to me. It's three light high notes over and over, but then her left hand suddenly starts heavy on the opposite side and I do feel a little sense of a shadow passing over. She continues this way, her arms at opposite ends, and it amazes me that she can play in such duology – deep bellows one side, light trippy notes on the other.

When she finishes, she turns to me. 'You have no idea what that was, do you?'

I shake my head.

'Michael Myers' theme song from *Halloween*, by composer John Carpenter.'

'I'll add it to the movies list,' I say and she nods.

'Why do you like this so much?' When she asks what I mean, and confirms I'm not talking about me, by giving me a quick and hard kiss, I explain. 'No, I mean – the horror music side of things. Why – this?'

'I love how music makes us feel. I mean, I bet lots of people have never actually seen *The Exorcist* or *Jaws* – but the second someone hears that Mike Oldfield music, they'll feel ice along their spine. Or they hear John Williams' two-note ostinato and have this impulse to *get out of the water*!'

And then she demonstrates. *The Exorcist* theme is indeed one I've heard before, even though I can't place where. I know it's horror and something to do with the devil. The same with *Jaws* – I know it's to do with a shark in the water.

'And it's always such smart composition. Because so much of horror-movie scoring is about the absence of sound. It's like . . . the musical equivalent of holding your breath, or straining to hear something go bump in the night. Then all of a sudden – *BOOM!* or *SCREECH* – the *Psycho!* strings. It's also all about repetition to mimic human reactions, like the simple alternating pattern of two notes – E and F, F and F sharp – for the *Jaws* theme, kind of feels like a racing heart.'

She starts playing the song from before – the one from *Halloween* – of the repeated three notes at opposite ends of the keys. 'Close your eyes,' she says, and I do. 'What does this sound like to you?'

But after a while I shrug, not sure – open my eyes only to have her tell me to close them again.

'What if I tell you that the *Halloween* movie is all about this girl Laurie. Imagine her walking home alone,' Ellie repeats the light, trippy three notes, 'and then she feels the presence of someone, maybe following her.' The heavier three notes come in. 'He's keeping pace but walking a distance behind, keeping her in his sights . . .' The same three notes running together really do sound like one is stalking the other.

'Okay, that's *so* creepy!'

Riya does the same riff, and even though I didn't know the story behind the music a minute ago, I do feel an inadvertent tingle down my spine listening to it now. It's a strange sensation, and it makes me wonder something else. 'I just don't know why anyone would want to feel that way.'

Riya smiles but doesn't stop playing. 'What do you mean?'

I shrug. 'I mean – why would you voluntarily scare yourself? Everything in horror down to the music is designed to make you paranoid and fearful and I just don't know why you'd want to feel that way . . . and it lingers? After watching *Tigers Are Not Afraid*, I did find myself staring at dark corners of my room at night, and not wanting to stick my foot out from the covers in case some bloody ghost hand grabbed it!'

She lets out a burst of laughter. 'That is a very common feeling of paranoia after watching horror.' I continue to stare at her with eyes that say *exactly!* She stops playing and swivels on the chair to face me. I mimic her too, so that the caps of our knees are just touching.

'I think – aside from the adrenaline rush and vicarious feeling of surviving something just like the characters after you've watched a scary movie – I think I love horror so much because the whole world can be one big scary place and especially for women, right?' Riya carelessly flicks her plait, and brushes stray curls away from her face – something I'm beginning to notice she does when she's excited. 'But there's something freeing about choosing to walk into a dark cinema and be scared. To take control and let yourself to be frightened, to give yourself over to it. Because we don't get a lot of say in what happens to us in the real world and the times we're scared when we don't want to be. Because there's some creep on a train brushing up against you, or some perv at a party who thinks you being wasted is a free pass . . .'

In my head I think, *Or some adults who think your fear is entertainment, that your vulnerability is their artistic vision brought to life.*

Riya continues, 'But *choosing* fear? In a controlled environment, where the stories can push us to think about what we'd do in that situation – especially when most of the time the hero in a horror film is a woman – that's amazing! That's powerful.'

I raise an eyebrow. 'You don't think other genres are as progressive and powerful? Like romantic comedies, or . . .'

Before I can think of more Riya has an answer. 'Sure, but I think that love sustains us, while fear reveals who we really are.'

'Lottie would have loved talking to you,' I say suddenly, and blink at the awareness of how true that is. Lottie loved people who appreciated and respected art, in all its forms.

Riya cracks a smile that's so wide and reaches her eyes. So I have to cup her face and kiss her lips because I have no resistance to this. But then as we pull apart somebody clears their throat behind us, and we both spin around.

'Mum!'

'Hello,' she says, and there's ice in her voice.

She's standing there, arms crossed and frowning at me and we both jump up from our seat at the piano. Riya even self-consciously smooths her school dress down.

'I didn't know you'd have company,' Mum says, slowly, enunciating each word.

'Mum, this is Riya Vaidhyanathan, and she's . . .' But I realise I don't know how to explain to Mum who Riya is without her being even angrier with me.

It's Riya who steps in. 'Hello, Ms Marsden. It's a pleasure to meet you.' She waves from where she's standing.

I think I've just about got the courage to say something resembling an explanation when Poe comes to the doorway to stand beside Mum and says the words that make her face purse up like she's just sucked on a lemon drop. 'Riya – hello, nice to see you again!'

Mum looks to Poe with narrowed eyes of realisation, and then back at me to say 'Ellie,' and then she's spinning on her heel and walking away, expecting me to follow her.

I turn to Riya and find that the smile has well and truly left her eyes as she looks at me sadly.

'She doesn't know about me, huh?'

I open my mouth to say something, but Riya waves me away. 'It's cool. I have to go anyway – school and all.'

'Riya, it's not what you think.' But I realise I can't tell her about the layers behind this grievance, because they all lead back to the reasons I've been mad and hurt by Lottie. The ways my family couldn't – wouldn't – protect me, and why I've found this world to be so scary.

I reach out a hand to Riya but she side-steps me and heads towards Poe and the doorway, saying over her shoulder, 'It's fine.' But from the flattened tone of her voice, I know it's not. And the look Poe gives me as he steps down into the conservatory to let Riya pass reenforces for me that it's definitely not okay.

'I'll show you out . . .' he says sadly, following after Riya – but not before he raises his eyes to the ceiling and then back at me, letting me know the way Mum has headed, and where I need to go.

TWENTY-EIGHT

I find Mum in the library, rifling through one of the drawers of a study table.

'Mum . . .'

'I am looking for your *bubbe*'s birth certificate. I don't suppose you've seen it?'

I shake my head no, and Mum continues to rummage.

'Mum, I met Riya through this film club which is a long story, but you should know,' I wish she'd stand still for a second, or at least turn and look at me, 'she knows everything – about Lottie.'

She stops moving and turns very slowly to me.

'What?'

'I told her because I trust her, and Yael agrees that . . .'

Mum cuts me off. 'Yael knows about Riya?!'

I wince momentarily at my slip-up, then nod my head slowly. What follows is a word-vomit that's part-explanation of my reasoning, mixed in with a brief run-down of mine and Riya's history up to this point. By the end I'm almost breathless, and Mum is still only looking at me with her blank face of disappointment.

'Mum – say something, please.'

'I don't know what to say.'

And I don't even want to think it, but I have to ask. 'This isn't because she's a girl, is it? Because I thought you and Dad understood, when I told you I was bisexual . . .'

At this, Mum scoffs and rolls her eyes. 'Ellie, give me a little more credit than that, please!'

I throw my hands up. 'Then what? What? I trust this person, I wanted her to know – I *needed* her to know – because I could be . . .' once I say this, there's no going back, so I take a deep breath, 'I could maybe be falling for her.'

At this, Mum all but yells, 'Then why didn't you tell me?!'

I stare at Mum for a beat and then through gritted teeth I say, 'Really? After what you said to me the other day? We haven't been speaking, Mum! I was hardly going to come out and have a heart-to-heart with you . . .'

Her face crumples, that's the only word for it. And then she walks over to the green chesterfield and all but collapses to sit down. I go to follow her, just as she says, 'You told him though, didn't you?'

Ah. Of course she'd be upset over that part. 'Poe?'

Mum nods, and I go to sit on one end of the lounge.

'I did, yes.'

She takes a deep breath. 'I don't understand why you never blamed him, but all of a sudden I'm the villain because I wanted peace with my mother, and for you to forgive her too . . .' She shakes her head. 'Poe never blamed her either, you know. They kept up their relationship even when you cut ties with her, so I don't understand.'

I sigh. 'Because Poe never tried to rewrite history and recast her as the victim. He always believed me, and I know he and Lottie had a rocky relationship after I told you all what happened. He never forgave her on my behalf, Mum. He never stopped believing me just because enough time had passed . . .' I shake my head. 'Since I've been back, I've been remembering the old Lottie, the one I grew up with. The one who encouraged me to daydream and dress up, who'd pass on the family stories and legends, who was happy that I was happy when I started getting into acting properly.' I pause for a moment, centring myself before adding, 'And how she hurt me, on that movie and after – when she didn't believe me, wouldn't accept that I was still being traumatised by that film, but in new ways.'

I reach out, and gently take my mum's hand – and then I squeeze. 'Both things are true, and both versions of Lottie exist. And I think the same way I have to remember that Lottie is more than that betrayal . . . I think maybe we both have to learn that we can still love her, even if we never stop being angry and hurt by her too.' I shrug. 'Death doesn't clean her of that.'

Mum lets out a shaky breath. 'When did you get so wise?' And then she squeezes my hand again. 'You're right. I wanted to forget, and I wanted you to forget that awful time. I thought absolving was the same as forgiving, but it's not. It's harder to go on loving someone even when they've hurt you, and I think I've been scared that you'll realise I've been to blame this whole time too . . .'

'Mum,' I say but she won't let me continue.

'I was so proud of your talent – your dad I both were. *Are*,' she corrects herself and continues. 'It was like you got both barrels of Lottie and Harvey. And I never wanted to hold you back so when Lottie came along with this script, I thought I had to let you go all in. For me and your dad to get out of your way and see if you really had the knack.'

She laughs, but not like anything is funny. 'And you did, kiddo – you were spectacular. Everyone said so, and your dad couldn't believe it either. But then when you told us how they did those scenes, how they got you to those places . . .' She shakes her head. 'Your father was so angry, and I was furious. I wanted to kill somebody. Because you're *my kid*. And I let you down too.'

I'm crying now, and Mum reaches over to tuck her hand underneath my chin and make me look at her. 'We should have gone to the police for you. We should have held firm with your old school, and insisted that those students were the problem, not you. And we should have spoken out about what that director did. I'm sorry we didn't. I'm sorry if that ever made you wonder if we believed you . . . but Lottie begged us not to.'

I suck in a sharp breath.

'She said the scandal would haunt you more than the moment. She said it was just the methods they used to get the best out of child actors.' She hangs her head. 'Your dad was insisting on going to the press, telling everyone – but then Lottie said there'd be no repercussions, all the blame would fall on her, and . . . you'd be the story, not what they did to you.'

My breathing quickens, my heart gallops and I need to close my eyes against the wave of nausea I feel.

'We're to blame too, and I'm so sorry, Ellie, more than you'll ever know.'

I slowly unclasp my hand from Mum's and pull it away. Then I rise and walk to the door, where I find Yael and Poe waiting for me.

They heard everything, by the looks on their faces – and by Yael opening her arms for me to fall into. The feel of Poe's hand gently cradling the back of my head, as I cry into Yael's neck.

TWENTY-NINE

A few hours later and I'm sitting in St David's Park with Yael, in the rotunda there. Riya is on her way to meet me but it's drizzling, and I feel guilty because I begged her to come and see me after school, even though I could hear in her voice that she was still hurt and reluctant.

'You sure about this?' Yael asks, almost like she read my mind.

I look out into the distance, and through the static of misting rain I can just make out Riya's purple jacket. She's carrying a yellow umbrella and heading our way.

I turn to Yael and try to smile. 'She's the only thing that makes sense right now. And I think I need her to see the real me . . . all parts of myself.' Even the ones I've been hiding.

Yael nods, then comes over to give me a one-armed hug before walking down the steps of the rotunda and raising her own umbrella, a clear plastic vintage bubble shape from the 60s with a flower pattern. I watch her walk along the same path Riya is on, and the two stop briefly. I wonder what they say, but then Yael reaches out to squeeze Riya's shoulder. Then she keeps walking away, back to the carpark on the other side of St David's, where she'll sit and wait for me in Harvey's old car.

And then Riya is walking up the large rotunda stairs. She closes her umbrella and shakes herself for a second, undoes the buttons on her jacket and then comes to me.

'Hi,' she whispers, and I say hi back, softly.

There are no chairs or bench seats in the rotunda. It's literally just a plain dome roof with strange blue-wooded ceiling, hexagon railing and columns all around. But the roof has a little extra lip on it, so we can perch facing each other with our back against a column. We tuck our feet into the trellis design to help balance us and we don't get a single drop of rain on us. We look out at the beautiful greenery of St David's Park lapping up the rain that's falling all around, and even pattering gently on the roof, and none of it touches us.

From here I can just see one side of the hospital, visible through the trees. I point it out to Riya, tell her that's where Lottie is right now.

We're quiet for a bit, just the rain speaks for us until I'm ready to. 'Speaking of my grandmother . . .' I begin, and then I stop because I don't know how to start. And then I realise it's Riya I'm talking to, so I decide to come at it from the side she knows best. 'I've never seen the movie we were in together, *Blood & Jacaranda*.'

It works. She's so surprised it breaks her silence and she lets out a surprised 'What?'

'That's why I couldn't talk about it for FNFG. I've never seen it. And the thing is – I don't want to.'

Riya waits for me, lets me talk.

'I really liked stories, growing up – which sounds lame. What kid doesn't? But I loved dressing up and playing make-believe, and I could have these long-running, epic dramas that would take up days and weeks playing by myself or with Yael, all over Lovinger House. And I loved watching Lottie in her movies, and for a long time I thought that was her in "real life", as I called it. But when I learnt that she was acting, that it was her playing make-believe on TV? *Well*, I was hooked. I wanted in.

'But Mum and Dad resisted for a really long time. Both of them know the industry and how tough it can be, and even though Lottie told them I'd enjoy dabbling, they kind of brushed away my interest. And then when I kept it up, they let me join the Hobart Children's Theatre. And I loved it – twice a week rehearsal after school, a play put on every three months. I loved all of it. I was only ten but I knew it was exactly what I wanted to be doing.

'And I remember after this one particular play, Lottie came backstage to tell me I'd done good. And the way she said it, I knew she meant it. I didn't know why, I had maybe – two lines? But I was on stage for a few acts . . . Anyway, it was a few months after she saw me in that play that she came to my parents and said she had a script for me. They'd all but dried up for her, by then – but this one landed on her desk and she knew it was something good. Something great. And they needed a kid . . .

'I don't really know what they spoke about or how she convinced them – but I know I wanted it so bad, and I was ten going on eleven. I knew my own mind! So when Lottie said they had to step back and let me try, they did. And anyway, she said if I was going to bomb out, better it be in a low-budget indie that nobody was likely to see.'

I look off in the distance, spy the random headstones and monuments in the gardens here, a reminder that the dead are near.

'Do you want to know the quickest way to ruin someone's childhood?' I don't wait for an answer, and I don't look at Riya as I say, 'You make them believe that they are a monster, and then you tear away the mask.'

Riya jumps down from her place on the ledge and walks over to me. I stay where I am, but I take her hand when she offers it.

'Little things at first. They locked me in my trailer for a couple hours one day, because they claimed the lock was jammed. It was fine, I mean – it was a small, dingy rented caravan – but it was okay. They got me out. Except it happened again a few days later, when I was in full prosthetics. That stuff was glued to my face, I couldn't take it off – an entire layer of silicone and rubber and I-don't-know-what, sitting on my face with white contacts in that I couldn't take out, that were burning my eyes by then. I had a full-blown panic attack, and that was when the door magically busted open.'

Riya breathes, 'Oh my God . . .' and I go on.

'And then it was the rumours too. Weird stuff the make-up ladies would say to me, about how the director had overheard Lottie talking about me. That I needed to run my lines more because I was mucking up. I knew my lines backwards and forwards, never mind that I didn't have many – that was the whole point! It was mostly physical, but I became obsessive about them. And even when I'd swear I'd hit it word perfect, the director would *cut* and tell me I'd missed a word or changed emphasis or something. Just to mess with me. And so the rumours grew that Lottie was angry with me. That I was wasting time and making her look bad. That she was ashamed. I got so nervous during takes that I'd totally flub my lines, and then I'd panic that everyone hated me – that Lottie was angry with me! And I'd be unable to get through them another time.'

Riya squeezes my hand.

'Of course, they kept running the camera as I had my meltdowns and panic attacks. When I apologised profusely, when Lottie would come on set just to stare me down behind the camera, they used it all. That was the point – how they got the scene just right.'

I squeeze back, when I begin on the end.

'And of course all those times my trailer door jammed, it all made sense when they decided to change up the finale and have it all end in a dark cave in the middle of nowhere and do some hand-held shooting, just me and Rob – the director. They set up those cameras so I couldn't see them – not in the dark – and then just left me there to freak out, to have a full-blown meltdown for the final scene. The one everyone talks about. That's just . . . *me.* No acting required.'

When I finish, I'm not crying – but Riya is. She wraps her arms around my middle and buries her head in my waist, so I turn a little more into her and stroke her hair.

'I didn't know the movie would take off like it did, and I'd have this memory of my torture blasted all around the world for people's entertainment. And then the stuff at school brought it all back and I couldn't go on pretending I was fine. So I left, finally.'

'Oh my gosh, the film club! Ellie, I'm so sorry . . .' Riya begins to say, and I squeeze her shoulders before hopping down from the railing, standing to face her.

'It's okay. You didn't know – we didn't tell anyone. Which I didn't even think about – why would I? I was a kid. Lottie twisted my memories of that time. She'd say she didn't know what had gone on, that I didn't confide in her – and then she'd change the excuse again, and say that those were just the methods they used to get me in the right headspace for the scene . . . I told my parents, but only once the movie had been out for a year, and the bullying at school had happened. That was my breaking point, when everything came out. And they were so angry – but they still didn't tell anyone. And I've just found out that was because of Lottie too.'

Riya sucks in a breath. I don't stop.

'The movie became her big moment, her re-entry back into that world . . . and it started making money, I guess. The whole family told me to just shut up and take it, effectively. Well, except for Poe and my parents.' I shake my head. 'So I left. Refused to talk to Lottie, didn't talk to a lot of the family, actually.'

'Until now,' Riya guesses, and I confirm.

'Until now.'

Riya breathes deeply and comes to stand beside me, both of us with our backs to the railing.

'That is so twisted.'

'I know.'

'No, Ellie – they abused you! And she *let* them!'

They did. She did.

I shrug. 'That's why my mum didn't know about you. She and I had this argument because she was rehashing all Lottie's old excuses, making me feel like I was misremembering or making a big deal over nothing . . . We weren't talking, and that's when you and I –' Here I wave a hand between us, to signify *us* and Riya nods in understanding.

I let out a ragged breath. 'You know what I found out years later?' Riya shakes her head. 'They did the same thing to Shirley Temple. And I'm not *comparing* myself to her fame or anything. But . . . one of her co-stars revealed that the way directors used to get Temple to cry on cue was to hide her mother on set, and then whisper in Shirley's ear that she'd been kidnapped by a man with blood-red eyes – and then keep the cameras rolling.'

Riya leans her shoulder against mine, and I'm thankful for the weight of her beside me.

'I'm not excusing it, but knowing I was one in a long line – because there are *so many* other stories of so many other actors – well . . . it helped a little. They didn't just do it to me because I wasn't good enough.'

Riya looks away for a second, I think to catch her breath or compose herself or something. Then she asks, 'Ellie, will you tell people? The authorities, or the media? You can still make them pay for what they did to you, and make sure they don't do it to anyone else.'

I nod slowly; 'I've been thinking about it, and I want to,' I frown. 'I *will*. Maybe it sounds pathetic but I've so wanted distance from what happened that I just didn't want to think about it. But I want to take back that control. I want to change my story.'

Saying this part out loud makes me think on another question. One that might be hard for Riya to comprehend. But I need to know.

'Riya – was it any good?'

She turns to me, her face a little horrified. 'What?'

'The movie, my role – I guess? Tell me. Was it worth it?'

She's shaking her head. 'Ellie, *nothing* is worth what happened to you!'

That's not what I meant. Not exactly. Of course I know that *logically.* But I'm still curious. Before I can ask again though, Riya is trying to explain.

'Separate the art from the artist, right? One should not impact the other but that's not true, Ellie – it's just not! There is no argument in which it's okay to support what happened to you, by in any way endorsing that movie!'

Then Riya reaches down and takes my hand, squeezes it once and doesn't let go. So I feel safe enough to say the next part.

'I guess I also want to know if it was worth Lottie sacrificing me, *us* – all our memories and relationship.' I breathe deeply, remembering Yael telling me that Lottie had once said that. *She'd regretted the sacrifices she'd made.*

'And I wish I'd come back sooner. I wish I'd spoken to her – to everyone. I wish I'd yelled and screamed and stayed and fought, because I have all these questions only she can answer, and it feels like I'll never get the ending I keep looking for. Hoping for . . .'

With our hands still clasped, Riya turns to me and I fold into her, placing my head in the crook of her neck and feeling her arms wrap around me.

THIRTY

The next morning Yael and I wake to the sound of yelling coming from downstairs. Voices travel up the wind-tunnel hallway to the second-floor bedrooms.

We meet in the hall, both of us poking our sleepy heads out from our doorways and sharing looks of confusion before more yelling carries through.

'*How dare you!*' The distinctive voice of my mother, followed by the deep baritone of Poe, but we can't make out what he's saying.

Yael and I link arms and then make our way downstairs. Yael is in a silky two-piece collared pyjamas set, and I'm in my oversized Sailor Moon t-shirt that goes down to my knees.

When we get to the bottom of the stairs the uncles Tobin and Seth are hastily pulling on coats and shoes. 'Maybe best if you come into town with us for a bit?' Seth says, grimacing as my mother's high-pitched '*That's rich, coming from you!*' rebounds around the room.

Yael shakes her head, and then pulls me along towards the kitchen. We hear the front door open and close behind us, and then we're looking at the scene before us.

Poe is sitting down at the breakfast nook, his shoulders hunched and arms crossed on the table in front of him. My mum is by the window on the far side of the room, the one looking out over the garden but with her back to the view as she leans against the bench with her arms crossed in front of her.

'What's going on?' Yael asks, looking back and forth between them.

I unlink our arms and go to stand by Poe, rest a hand gently on his shoulder and ask, 'Are you okay?'

My mother scoffs from the other side of the room, unamused – but there's also a hurt there too. 'Of course, forever the favourite,' she says under her breath, but intending us to hear.

'Please, Louise . . .' Poe begins, but my mother shakes her head.

'I screwed up. I hate myself for it – but I learnt to keep secrets in this family because of you,' my mum's words spit fire at him.

'What?' Yael asks, just as Poe says, 'I never wanted that . . .'

'What are you talking about?' I repeat Yael's question.

Mum shakes her head again, laughs under her breath – but not like anything is actually funny. 'It's pretty rich when everyone's favourite comes to me to say we need to confront the past head-on, no more secrets, clean slate, because that's what Lottie would want . . .'

Yael hedges closer to me and Poe, and we both look back and forth between them as Mum goes on.

'Favourite relative, favourite person, favourite human – you're all just like Lottie and Harvey in that regard.'

At this, I truly don't know what she means. But I take a guess. 'Mum – did you think Lottie loved Poe more than you, or something?'

Poe makes a move as though he's going to rise from his seat, but then Mum pushes herself off from the counter and takes a few steps closer, her arms still crossed as she says, 'I think Lottie and my dad both did.'

There's silence in the kitchen, and then Poe slumps into his seat once again and I remove my hand from his shoulder as I keep my eyes on Mum.

It's Yael who clears her throat and asks, 'Are you saying that – that Poe and Harvey . . .'

Mum nods once. 'I don't know how deeply you'd have to dig into search engines, but there are enough old gossip columns floating around from that time. And I have my own memories, of course.'

Yael takes a deep breath, and then walks slowly to the other side of the breakfast table and pulls out a seat. She lands on the wooden chair with an audible thud and places her clasped hands on the table in front of her. 'Whoa,' she says.

I step back from Poe in order to look at him, his hunched shoulders and downcast eyes, he's very still.

Yael clears her throat to ask, 'So all three of them . . . ?'

And Poe lets out a bark of laughter that makes me and Yael jump, and has him slapping his big hand over his mouth instantly, even as I can see his eyes are tearing up from trying to keep more laughter in.

From where we're each situated around the kitchen, Mum, Yael and I all watch in stupefied silence as Poe's whole body shakes from withheld laughter, and then as he waves a hand, as though asking us to give him a moment to collect himself.

He eventually wipes his eyes and takes a deep breath before looking at Yael very seriously. 'No, we three were best friends. They were my favourite people in all the world . . . but Harvey and I were more than that, always were.' He smiles, but still shakes his head. 'It was a very different time back then. And Harvey Hutton – *the* Harvey Hutton – had an image he was trying to project and protect. So he married Lottie.' He lifts his eyes to look at my mum, and I don't turn around to see her reaction. I keep my eyes on Poe.

'They made it work – even though they loved each other very differently to how Harvey and I . . .' Poe waves the thought away, 'and they had you, together – and you made them *so* happy.'

My mum makes a noise behind me, and I turn around to see her arms are hanging by her sides and there's tears in her eyes as she stares at Poe. And I don't even think, I just move and go to throw an arm around her shoulders and squeeze.

'Aunt Louise, you knew all this?' Yael asks, gently. 'I thought you could barely remember your dad . . . ?'

'I remembered a few things, not much but – enough. And it all came out when we fought over you, and what she let happen,' Mum says, and I loosen her from my one-armed hug so she can turn to me. 'She went on and on about the sacrifices you have to make in life in order to be an artist. I got pretty angry with her, that she considered you – *my kid*, her granddaughter – a sacrifice for her career, and then she told me our entire family was built on sacrifice.'

My mum takes a deep breath and I let my arm fall away completely. 'I think she was shocked that she told me that way. In the middle of a fight . . . she wanted to sit down and explain, but

I bolted. And then we didn't speak for a year – after everything – but she really wanted me to know, to set the story straight. How much she loved Poe and Harvey, how dear they were as friends – and how much she wanted to have kids, but never thought she'd find someone she loved as much as Harvey, even if he couldn't love her back in quite the same way. And then how you and her found comfort in each other,' she says, looking to Poe briefly. 'She wrote it all down in a letter and when I finally read it,' Mum sniffs and shakes her head, 'Ellie, it's part of the reason I had to go some ways to forgiving her. But she didn't want anyone else in the family to know.'

'Seems to be a theme of hers.'

Mum gives a waterlogged laugh. 'And as for me and Poe . . . Once Lottie told me everything, memories came flooding back. What I thought were half-remembered dreams were really memories. And I don't like this about myself, but I guess I have to admit that even when I was a little girl – half knowing what I did – I knew my dad drank because he was unhappy, and he was unhappy because he was always hiding something. And Poe was his secret.'

Poe rises from his seat then and walks slowly towards Mum. She could turn away or step back from him, but she doesn't. Not even when he reaches out with his big hands to gently cup her face and run his thumbs beneath her eyes – brushing aside the tears.

'I didn't know she'd told you,' he says.

'I asked her not to,' she whispers back, and Poe's hands fall.

'I thought we'd have time . . . it was so much, and I wanted to come home and talk to you both,' Mum shakes her head, 'But we ran out of time, is all.'

'Not all of us.'

Mum starts crying again. 'I've been so awful to you; you loved him, but I didn't know! All this time I thought you were trying to take him away from us, that you made his life harder . . .'

Poe throws his arms around Mum and she sobs into his shirt as he gently pats her back. But eventually he pulls away to look at her, and say, 'I think you'll find that we were the ones who helped him be himself, Louise – you, me, and Lottie – we weren't the burdens he was carrying.'

I walk to where Yael is still sitting, gobsmacked, and place a hand on her shoulder which she reaches up to hold, tightly. 'This family is *wild*,' she says, and squeezes.

THIRTY-ONE

I didn't think I could, but I go back to the hospital to sit by Lottie. It's been a few days since I've been here with her. Mum and Poe both said I didn't have to. Yael offered to sit with me – but I said I wanted to be here. By myself. Even as I also texted Riya, and last night told her the deep dark thing I hadn't wanted to examine too closely; this feeling and fear I had that my withholding forgiveness was a tether. Like my anger was keeping her here, and maybe just moving on was a sacrifice I had to make for her sake.

Riya had called me as soon as she'd finished reading that message.

'Ellie.' She'd breathed my name with such sympathy, I started to cry.

'You know you're allowed to feel this way, right? She hurt you, and you're allowed to be angry. You're also allowed to still love and miss her when she's gone – none of this is wrong.' Riya was silent for a bit, listening to my muffled crying.

Eventually I was able to take a few shaky breaths and say, 'I've been thinking a lot about what comes next. When she's not here, but I'll have to start talking about and confronting what happened. And I know it's ridiculous, but even thinking about how much this will affect other people and how they'll react makes me hyperventilate and want to hide.'

'What other people? The ones who should be held accountable, because . . .'

I shook my head, then realised we're on the phone so I told her *no*; explained. 'It's like you said the other day, the *separate the art from the artist* thing and how much Lottie means to people – meant to people – how much our movie did too.' I took another deep breath. 'I mean – it's the reason I met you. That you wanted to know me . . .'

Riya was quiet for a bit, and my heart was beating fast waiting for her.

'That's true. But it's not all of you, Ellie – it's not the reason I . . .' she paused, and I wondered what she was going to say but she was already continuing. 'It's not the reason for you and me. You are so much more than that, and we are too. But the same way forgiveness doesn't mean forgetting, we can accept that we wouldn't have met had it not been for that film bringing us together, and people will see that they can still love something even if it means knowing an uglier truth behind its creation.' Riya took another deep breath. 'Besides, the thing that people most cling to isn't the product of art, but the messages it instils.'

I'd let out a slightly waterlogged laugh. 'Well then, I'm doomed. I'm not so sure there's anything worthwhile to have learned from our film.'

I'd suddenly felt exhausted after that. Even as I could tell that Riya wanted to keep talking, I had to beg off, explaining that I was sitting with Lottie tomorrow morning and felt like I needed to get some rest and be mentally ready.

I'd been right, as it turns out. But nothing could have prepared me for the shock of walking into her hospital room.

She's . . . sunken. Gaunt and her skin translucent, like she could break apart at any moment. When I arrived, I stalled in the doorway, and Corinne must have understood the shocked look on my face. She gently told me that she thought the end would come soon.

I also noticed a chill in the room, and Corinne guiltily admitted to me that she opened the window for a few minutes, and the reason why.

'Don't laugh, and don't think I'm loopy, but – I've been doing this for a while now, and I just think there's something about needing an open window for when the time comes. For their spirit, or soul or – *whatever* you want to call it. I just thought I'd see if she was ready.'

I didn't laugh or think Corinne was loopy. Instead, I told her, 'You know, in a Jewish house of mourning you shroud all the mirrors. It's because there's no vanity in grief, but I've always thought that maybe there's something more mystical to it . . . like a mirror could be a place where a departing spirit could get trapped, mistaking the reflection for the world they're meant to be leaving. Or something.'

Corinne seemed to relax. She cranked the up wall-heater and left the room. But it got me thinking – about what a soul needs to depart.

And then my phone rings, and it's Riya.

'Hi, it's you,' I say, smiling.

'It's me.' Then she takes a deep breath and says, 'and I'm at the hospital.'

I blink and begin to try to wrap my head around this, but Riya continues. 'Well, technically I'm in the hospital carpark, and I was wondering . . . do you think you could come down and meet me?'

I get up and walk to the doorway, stick my head out and see Corinne at the nurse's station, and then say to Riya, 'Give me ten minutes?'

It's a cloudy day in Hobart, the sky is looking like more rain is only a minute away. I ask Corinne to sit with Lottie while I quickly run an errand, and she agrees. So I jog down to the hospital carpark and scan the spaces – until I spot Riya's red Volkswagen Jetta. The windows are cracked, which also helps in finding her as I can hear the faint sound of Radio Tehran, which I recognise from the *A Girl Walks Home Alone at Night* soundtrack.

I walk up to the passenger side and rap twice on the window, the music turns off and the door unlocks. I slide in.

'Hi?' I say, a little perplexed.

Riya is unbuckled, so leans over and kisses me, quick. 'Hi.'

We both speak at once.

'What are you –'

'I'm sorry, I know –'

We both smile awkwardly, and then I wave for her to continue.

'I know it's important for you to be with your grandmother right now. But I kept thinking about what you said last night, and . . .' Riya takes a deep breath, and then looks at me very seriously as she says, 'I practised this last night and I just want to get it out, okay?'

I nod, and she starts talking.

'*Blood & Jacaranda* put an old spin on new frustrations; different topics, but the same battle – essentially generational. It was iconic having Lottie Lovinger in a clash with her own granddaughter, refusing to do what is right for her. Killing her slowly instead. Lots of people have read modern-day child activists into that, from climate change to gun control – the whole idea that the film is a "coming of rage" from the point of view of the monster really spoke to people. And to have Little Mate survive – not be killed or sacrificed like so many other monsters . . . it made audiences reconsider who the real hero of the story was. That maybe a monster could be both.'

I can only stare at her, and feel a little frown forming between my brows before she's reaching over and taking one of my hands in hers, and squeezing.

'It was good, and you were great – but that's still not worth the sacrifice, and people who claim that it's important and revelatory, who say they know its deeper meaning, will see that.' She smiles gently. 'And if they don't, then they never really understood it in the first place.'

'That is . . .' I begin, not sure if I have the words, but then Riya's eyes go wide and she's out of her seat, butt in the air, as she dives behind me for her backpack. She retrieves an eggshell-coloured envelope that she holds aloft and then out to me.

'One more thing,' she says. 'You kept talking about sacrifice – and it got me remembering something I'd read, that I think you should keep.' I accept the envelope from her.

'That's the letter the film club received, from Lottie – accepting our invitation.'

I turn it over in my hands and sure enough, there is my grandmother's perfectly neat script in dark blue ink. I must have a strange look on my face, because Riya says, 'Read it and you'll see.'

The rain is still falling, so Riya clicks her seatbelt on, starts her car, and drives me around to the entrance of the hospital, then turns to me once more. 'I'll be around if you want to talk later.'

I open the door and put one leg out, then look back at her. 'Thank you,' I say, and then I go.

THIRTY-TWO

Back in the room I take the same seat by Lottie, and gently open the envelope and pull out her letter, written on thick cream paper.

I begin reading as her machines keep beeping

Dear Ms Jones and Ms Vaidhyanathan,

I am writing to accept your offer of an appearance, as well as a question-and-answer segment following a screening of Blood & Jacaranda.

I have a great fondness for the State Cinema and will endeavour to play a small part to ensure its affiliated film club can continue to thrive and service its dedicated community of film-lovers. Especially those with such a commitment to making cinema-going accessible for more people and celebrating the feminist elements of the horror genre in particular.

Though I admit to being unsure if this particular film merits applause for exemplifying such qualities. I fear it is not deserving of the high esteem in which you and many others hold it.

And that may well be the biggest indication for me that it is time I started talking more honestly about my experiences and sacrifices in relation to this movie . . . especially if they force me to acknowledge the villainous role I played, in more ways than one.

Please feel free to call me on my private home line, written below, so that we may begin arrangements.

Yours sincerely,
Lottie Lovinger

I let out the breath I didn't realise I was holding, and then fold the letter neatly and slip it back into the envelope. I'm not crying, but I feel like I could at any moment.

'I don't know if you're holding on, because you're waiting for me to forgive you,' I say, then I hold the envelope up as though Lottie could see it. 'I don't know if this means you were ready to start talking honestly about what happened, and if so, I don't know what caused your change of heart.'

I lay the envelope back in my lap. 'But if it helps, and – I don't know – if this is a final concern that you need to be put away,' I roll my eyes a little at this, 'then just know that I love you. I always did; I always will. I'm still hurt by you, and mad at you – but I can forgive you. Because you are more than just your worst moments, *Bubbe*. And we had so many good ones too.'

And then I reach out and take her hand – gently hold it in my mine, for the first time in a long time.

THIRTY-THREE

Any lightness I feel over sitting and talking to Lottie, finally, is overrun the next morning, when news alerts start pinging our phones. Then Mum comes bursting into the kitchen to announce, 'The bastards know and they printed it.'

Suddenly we're all reaching for our devices, and I catch the headline briefly in my quick scroll, just as Jasper pulls his phone in front of him, and Yael reads over his shoulder, blinking at her father when he lets out a sudden expletive.

HOBART TOWN GAZETTE

'Screen Legend Lottie Lovinger Close to Death'

Mum brushes tears from her cheeks and says, 'All she asked, and we couldn't give her that.'

Tobin is scrolling, and then he and Poe read from his screen.

'This paper has learnt that local icon and screen legend Charlotte "Lottie" Lovinger has been on end-of-life care for close to a month now, following a stroke and bleed on the brain,' Tobin reads aloud, followed by his own expletives.

Jasper reads another section out. 'Lottie's publicist last month informed media outlets that her client had undergone surgery on her lymph nodes and was forced to retire early from the stage production that she also co-produced, *The Lion's Bride*. We now understand that this was deliberate misinformation to afford Ms Lovinger a modicum more privacy . . .' At this he tosses his phone on the table. 'Fat lot of good that did.'

My eyes are scanning my own screen when I catch sight of a familiar name and read that paragraph. *Lovinger's second and ex-husband, the Oscar-winning costume designer Poe Tuhana, is also reported to have been in town for a number of weeks as he keeps vigil by her bedside, along with the rest of the family. In keeping with Jewish customs, when the time comes Lovinger will reportedly be buried at . . .*

I can't read any more.

'Who told them?' Yael asks, from where she now sits on one side of the dining-room table.

'"A trusted source," is all they say,' Mum practically spits the words out.

'One of the actors looking for relevance and a little easy money?' my uncle Tobin poses, sounding painfully like the lawyer he is.

Jasper says, 'Nurses, doctors, hospital staff, janitors, a visitor happening to stroll by – it could have been anyone.'

'Louise, anyone you've contacted who couldn't be trusted? Anyone outside family and friends . . . ?' Tobin asks, and that sets my mum off.

It also makes me gulp down a bile of dread. Because the

thought just occurs to me. There is someone outside our immediate circle who knows.

Riya.

I don't want the thought to enter my body – but once it's in, it burrows deep. As does a memory of Riya saying that Ah-Pei's dad writes for the *Hobart Town Gazette.*

Yael catches my eye and I wonder if her mind has gone to the same place as mine. Is it because I expect to be betrayed by the people closest to me, or is it that constantly being betrayed by people I care about has me assuming the worst?

It's Poe who tries to calm everyone, by standing up and throwing his hands out – like he's surrendering, or refereeing. 'We all just need to . . .'

But it's no good. The skeletons are well and truly out of the closet, the gloves are off.

And the wolves are at the gate – literally.

Not just tourist buses anymore, but actual news vans and paparazzi are camped outside the Lovinger front gate. Seth arrives home from sitting with Lottie. He already knows what's happened from his phone and alerts for her name, the same we all had programmed. He warns us that they could have drone cameras flying overhead, so he has us close all the curtains so they can't peek in.

But we still need to be with Lottie – and so on Sunday we go three together, the car moving through the quicksand of a crowd, inching our way down the driveway, while one person with a hood down shuts the gate behind us and then quickly jumps back in.

The Sydney agents draw up a 'please respect our privacy at this time' plea that we all know none of them will heed. We also all agree to turn our phones off, and disconnect the landline in case any stray gossipmonger manages to find our numbers. Better to stonewall them, give them no oxygen. Part of me is also relieved to not to have to check and see if Riya has reached out, the paranoia of deciphering any messages she may send.

There's a little more decency and decorum at the hospital, but not much. And it's by luck and by law that they can't come onto her floor, but it still hurts when I hear Mum telling her that we couldn't fulfil one of the final wishes.

Two hours into sitting with her, when there's so little left of Lottie to see, it's Yael who finally asks me, 'What are you thinking?'

And I give her a look that she and Mum instantly interpret.

'Don't go there,' Yael says.

But I have to know.

Which is why I stay all day at the hospital – first sitting with Mum and Yael, then Poe and Seth. I even manage to take a one-hour nap on the trundle bed they put out for us when we stay overnight, listening to the sound of Bette Davis and Joan Crawford at each other's throats through *What Ever Happened to Baby Jane?* puts me right to sleep.

And then it's nearly time and I call a ride on the phone in Lottie's room and duck out via a smoker's entrance on a back stairwell to avoid anyone following me. I know I'm being paranoid, and logically if the culprit is someone at the film club, then they'll find me anyway.

When we pull up to the State Cinema, my stomach is in knots – until I step out, look around, and breathe a sigh of relief that there's no microphones or cameras in sight, except for the old-fashioned one positioned in one of the cinema windows as decoration.

The club must have already started, because there's no Riya at the box office – so I head downstairs and sure enough, the door to the usual cinema basement is closed. Club in session.

When I push it open, Jen and Riya are up the front talking. I just hear the tail-end of '. . . a stalking haunting,' when silence falls at the sight of me, and I watch as Riya's face seems to contort in pain. Or is it guilt?

Suddenly she's bounding down the aisle, talking rapidly as she approaches me. 'Ellie, I've been trying to call you all day but your phone is off – and I tried to come and see you, but there were all these . . .'

'Was it you?'

My words stop her dead, before she reaches me.

'What?'

I sniff and hold my ground. 'Was it you?'

When I ask it again, I see movement out the corner of my eye, and Ah-Pei is slowly standing, already has tears in her eyes.

'Ellie, I'm so sorry – I had no idea . . .'

'So that *was* your dad? *Hobart Town Gazette*, right?'

Ah-Pei's tears come quickly then, and it's Kate who stands up to throw an arm around her shoulders. 'She didn't know. She didn't know what he was doing!' says Kate.

I look back to Riya, whose face has turned ashen. 'So you told everyone, Ah-Pei told her dad and he, *what*? Ran with it?'

Riya starts shaking her head, slowly. Meanwhile Jen is at the front of the cinema still, madly signing and I see Maria from her seat is quickly catching her up.

'I wasn't . . . I didn't think –' she stammers, but I don't let Riya finish.

'This is my family, *my life*! How could you? How dare you?'

'Hey, Ellie,' Maria tries – but I don't let them finish. I don't let any of them finish, even when Riya starts crying and reaches out a hand. I step back, throw my hands in the air to wave her off. I notice she has two red love hearts as collar-tips, with a dagger through each. How fitting.

'I never should have trusted you.'

It's a little cliché, but it works as a departing line. I spin around and push back out the doors, race up the stairs and back out the front where the taxi is still waiting, helping me complete my dramatic exit almost perfectly.

Except for the way I curl into myself on the back seat and can't help but shake uncontrollably from the tears the whole way home.

THIRTY-FOUR

There's no sudden lack of oxygen this time, just the feeling of the blanket lifting and somebody climbing into bed fully clothed behind me. Cold, denim-clad legs spoon mine and Yael holds me as I cry some more.

After being unable to for so long, I'm a little disturbed at the development that I now can't seem to stop.

But eventually when I'm all cried out I roll over, to the inky outline of Yael's face in the dark.

'It was Riya.'

'What?!'

'I'm guessing she told film club, and one of the girls there – her dad wrote the article.'

'For the *Gazette*?' I nod my head, hoping Yael can see or feel the movement in the dark.

'But are you *sure*?'

'I told Mum. She's doing what she can to confirm.'

'Oh cousin, I'm so sorry.' And then Yael feels around for my hand in the dark, clasps it tight and brings them both to rest on the pillow between us.

When I wake in the morning, my hand is empty.

I wander downstairs to find Poe in the kitchen, and he tells me that Yael, my mum and Jasper all left for the hospital early.

'Yael told me your theory about Riya,' Poe says, as I take my first sip of tea. 'For what it's worth – I just don't see it being her. The way she looked at you, Ellie . . . I can't believe she'd do that.'

'Believe it.'

Poe puts his own cup of coffee down, and comes and leans on the kitchen island a little closer to me. 'Do you, really?'

I don't know what to say, so Poe keeps talking.

'Not everyone you love is going to hurt you, you know.'

I still don't say anything, and then I'm saved from having to by his phone ringing. Poe glances at the screen for a moment, just long enough that it screams again before he's pressing a button and bringing it to his ear, turning his back to me as he takes the call.

I listen to him say hello – and then no more. And my skin prickles.

Poe talks in a hushed voice into the phone, and I strain to hear. I put my cup of tea down and get off the tall kitchen stool.

'I'll bring her with me,' Poe says. He hangs up and turns around. And I already know what he's going to say. I can feel it, like a chill running down my spine – and Riya was right, the absence of sound is one of the most frightening things. If only because it makes room for what's coming . . .

THIRTY-FIVE

There are stages to mourning: *Aninut, Sheloshim, Shanah, Yahrzeit, Yizkor.*

In the first stage, mourning doesn't even exist yet. *Aninut.* We're too practical and there's too much to be done, so comfort can't begin until burial has been organised.

You're not supposed to comfort the *onen*, the mourner, during *Aninut*. But I wonder if because we're all *onen* in this house, that maybe the rules don't apply.

Which leads me to think that maybe there are no rules for dying.

I hug Yael and Mum to me when they get home, and it's Mum who clings to me longer, who burrows her face in my shoulder and just weeps. Her mum has died, and now she has no parents left. As I hold her, I can't wrap my head around how sad that must be, how much I can't comprehend it from this side.

Then the organising begins. The practicalities of *Aveilut* – mourning. My mum and three uncles will be *aviel* for one year. Mourners altered forever by their loss.

This time is a blur, even more so for the glare of the cameras that come and then go. There are stories about Lottie and announcements of her death, chronicles of her life. But we're all too busy and by the time we're in the third day of *shiva* – three of seven – the media has all but moved on.

It's on this day that Yael and I steal away to the blue room for a break. Our parents are sitting low to the ground and still receiving guests into the house – theatre community, industry people, the cousins from Queensland, even Kaleb ended up arriving today after all his bluster. There seems to be an endless stream of mourners needing greeting, and it's exhausting.

I collapse onto my bed, while Yael pulls out the little chair at the clamshell vanity. The entire mirror is currently draped in a black shroud. Then she swings around to look at me. I can feel her staring, so I swipe self-consciously at my face.

'What?'

'You do look like that actress.'

I sit up. 'Huh?'

'Simone Simon? From some movie about a horny jaguar?'

'Panther.'

'Whatever – the one Riya said you looked like.'

Hearing her name makes something clench in my heart.

'Well, you do look like her,' Yael finishes. 'I just realised I can see it.'

I keep staring at the rose plaster on the ceiling as I say the next part. 'Did you know, I learnt something about that movie?'

'Oh yeah?'

'Yeah – it does this Lewton's Law thing – to never reveal the monster. Named for Val Lewton, the screenwriter and producer.

Apparently, it was something he did in a lot of his movies, and it was definitely because they were low budget and they couldn't – you know – *afford* to have a panther trainer on set or whatever, and there was no CGI back then. Even the art on the movie poster was terrible.' I laugh at the memory of it hanging on Riya's wall. 'Clearly drawn at a time when you couldn't just Google "panther" and draw from a likeness. But I think he also did it because he trusted that whatever the monster was, the *idea* in audiences' imaginations would be so much scarier than anything they could come up with on screen.'

'He let their imaginations take over?'

'Yeah . . . it's kind of like, making room for silence because the unknown is where our fears mostly live.'

Yael gets up from the vanity to come and collapse on the bed with me. She's at the opposite end, so our heads are in the middle, with our legs hanging over the bed. Her cloud of hair is tamed in a discreet top-knot next to my more-gelled-than-usual-to-look-respectable red shag.

'You looked that all up, huh? Just for fun?'

I shrug into the mattress. But then Yael turns her head to me and I roll my eyes. 'Fine! I hunted down a copy of the movie online. I just wanted to watch it and see . . .'

'Do a little research on her first celebrity crush?'

Maybe. Maybe because a very small part of me missed the way she talked about movies, like they mattered. It was kind of intoxicating, being close to someone so passionate.

Yael gently bumps my shoulder. 'So what's your Lewton Law then?'

'Huh?'

'What's the monster you've never seen?'

I know exactly what the answer is, but before I can get the words out there's a loud *CRASH* from downstairs – the sound of glass shattering, strangely followed by a *DONG, DONG, DONG* of the grandfather clock striking.

Yael and I look at one another, but in a split second we're both standing and racing down the stairs – except we don't get very far before we have to stop. Because at the bottom in the entryway are Poe and it looks like Kaleb, and they've got each other in a headlock, with the grandfather clock fallen at their feet – glass crunching underfoot as they continue to scuffle.

'*Zeyde*?' Yael asks.

'Poe?' I say.

And we both watch the scene unfold and mourners start pouring out from every room in the house. They come from the front room where my mum and uncles were sitting *shiva* on low chairs, to the back, and the sunroom/kitchen where we had food and refreshments set up.

Poe and Kaleb are both breathing heavily, but Poe definitely has the advantage, even though there's maybe only a couple of years difference in their age. Poe is taller and broader, while Kaleb is squat and solid and they're both trying to use different tactics to get the upper hand.

Kaleb is reaching behind and trying to yank on Poe's shirt and navy blazer, which has the buttons done all the way up and is making his face bloom in suffocating red. Meanwhile Poe has an arm firmly around Kaleb's neck, and is trying to use his height to bend him lower to the ground. From the sounds he's making it's definitely putting a strain on his back. The grandfather clock has fallen like a beam across the starburst-tiled entryway in the kerfuffle.

It's my mum who manages to break through the crowd of the front sitting room. A sea of mourners parts for her when she makes a pathway with her arms and yells, 'Move, move, out of the way, what is going . . .'

And then she's at the threshold between the sitting room and hallway. She takes in Poe and Kaleb literally at loggerheads, but both of them flailing.

'Somebody *stop them*!' I yell, but most eyes of the mourners just look up at me.

Yael adds, '*Pull them apart*!'

But the mourners don't do anything and from up high on the stairs I can see the three uncles are now struggling to make their way through the crowd.

When nobody moves, it's my mum who springs into action – forever the problem-solver.

She picks up a massive blue-white patterned antique vase that's sitting on the side table. It's filled with water and a beautiful bouquet of native flowers sent by the Theatre Royal and put out by Mum, even though we don't really do flowers for funerals.

She plucks the flowers out and place them on the table, then walks calmly towards Kaleb and Poe. She gives them one last opportunity to break apart, and when they don't, she lifts the vase above their heads and tips the whole lot out. A salad's bowl worth of cold water lands on their heads and they spring apart quickly.

They both run hands down their faces and rub their eyes. Mum keeps a hold of the vase with one hand and puts another on her hip. This is also how her three brothers find her when they finally come through the crowd. Jasper goes straight to his father and places a hand on his shoulder, which Kaleb shrugs off aggressively.

'Now – *what is going on*?' Mum demands.

And it's Poe who speaks. 'He is not welcome here.'

I think Poe's about to take another swipe at him, but Seth suddenly jumps in between them and even throws his arms out to distance them.

'Poe, explain yourself!' Mum asks.

'It was him – he tipped off the papers.'

A gasp goes through the crowd.

'Is that true?' Jasper asks his father, and beside me Yael sinks down to sit on the step of the staircase we're standing on, and I do the same.

Kaleb is staring daggers all around, but he's not denying it either. It's Poe who keeps talking and explaining.

'I called in a favour at the local Hobart paper – but they'd only confirm it was someone close to the family and a reliable source. Unpaid tip-off, mind you – they wanted to stress that.' Poe adjusts his blazer and undoes the top button of his white shirt. His neck is red but the colour in his cheeks is coming down again. And honestly, when he runs his hands through his wet hair, he looks a little like he could be on a tasteful cover of *GQ*. 'By then I had an inkling and made a few more enquiries to confirm that the tip-off reached their paper's hotline from a Launceston location.'

Another gasp goes through the crowd, and beside me Yael huffs. 'Can our family go easy on the theatrics, just for *once*?'

By now, Kaleb is sputtering and lashing out. But it's Jasper who takes his father by the upper arm and muscles him towards the door. Tobin yanks it open and holds it for him so Jasper can fling him out and follow after, probably marching him down to the gate to make sure he's properly on his way.

It's Mum again who rallies everyone. 'That's the end of the show, folks. If you could all please disperse and let us get on with paying my *mame* the respect she deserves.'

I think the crowd of mourners is duly chastened, and so they hurry back to their respective corners. Tobin and Seth work together to lift the grandfather clock and get it upright. Then Tobin goes to look for a broom and dustpan for the glass while Seth goes into the front room to look after the crowd.

Poe and Mum both come to sit with Yael and me, a couple of steps down from us. Poe lets out a deep sigh and puts his elbows on his knees and holds his head in his hands. My mum looks off into the distance. I don't know if they're both about to laugh or cry, so I try to tip them towards one.

'Hanukkah is going to be very interesting this year.'

That does it. He and Yael both giggle and then outright laugh. Mum only sends me a tight smile, and once the other two die down she reaches behind her to take my hand and give it a squeeze. 'You know this means Riya had nothing to do with it. Just a sad coincidence that her friend's dad writes for that paper . . .' she says.

I do realise. I realised it as soon as Poe said what he did, and I felt my heart plummet. I think it's still somewhere at the bottom of the staircase, having rolled out from under me completely.

Yael takes my other hand and squeezes it, just as Poe spins around and gives me an apologetic but forceful smile. 'Take it from someone who daily wishes that he had more time with the people he loved.' At this, Mum reaches over with her other hand to place it gently on Poe's knee, and he smiles at her kindly. 'Apologise, be honest, tell her the demons you're wrestling with sometimes mean you don't see the world or people very clearly.'

'Grovel,' I say. 'I should also do some grovelling, right?'

All three of them nod their heads at me.

THIRTY-SIX

It's about to turn to dusk on Sunday afternoon, and Riya is at home.

In fact, I know she is because she wasn't at the State Cinema when I went to look for her earlier. The rest of the club were, though, and it felt like a particularly bad case of déjà vu when Yael and I burst into the room, only to find Jen at the front by herself.

'What do *you* want?' Maria asked, her voice distinctly chilled.

I turned my head and saw her, Kate and Ah-Pei on the couch – and Ah-Pei seemed to physically shrink away when my gaze landed on her.

'I'm looking for . . .' I began, but Jen started signing from where she was standing and Kate interpreted.

'She's not here, and she doesn't want to see you.'

I took a few more steps into the room, while Yael hung back by the door. 'I know, and I get that – I screwed up, big time.' I briefly glanced over my shoulder to make sure Kate was still interpreting for me, but when my eyes landed on Ah-Pei again I stopped walking and turned fully to address her. 'It's not your fault, I found out . . .'

'But my dad still wrote the article!' Ah-Pei blurted. 'And I'm *so sorry*, I didn't . . .'

I shook my head to cut her off. 'You shouldn't be made to feel bad for other people's actions, even the people you love. You are not defined by other people's mistakes.' And then I blinked at the words that just came out of my mouth.

I looked towards Yael, who gave me a patient smile – and then I turned back to Jen, who was looking at me closely and then signed something.

'You promise you won't make Riya cry?' Kate asked.

I thought for a minute. 'To the best of my ability.'

Which is how we've now come to be parked out the front of Riya's house – where I can hear the faint sound of instrumental music playing inside, and mango leaves and marigold flowers are hung around the door for Diwali that has fallen on this Sunday, as Jen and the club explained to me.

'What are you waiting for?' Yael asks, from all the way across on the bench seat, behind the steering wheel of Harvey's wagon.

Then a quote comes to mind, one I read recently, and that stuck with me. It's from *Frankenstein*: 'Beware; for I am fearless, and therefore powerful.'

I could do with a little of that monster-courage, and the absence of fear would come in handy. But if watching a small selection of horror movies has taught me anything, it's that you don't get to fearlessness or to be the Final Girl by waiting in the car. You get it by actually confronting the things that scare you and accepting the possibility that you could lose.

Which also reminds me . . .

'Hey.' Yael, who had turned to study Riya's house intently, turns back to me. We're both still in our respectable mourning wear. There's no Jewish custom to wear black – just that you have to keep wearing the same clothes to *shiva* as you wore to the funeral. I opted for a pair of navy culottes, and, in a tribute to Lottie's 70s style, a Marimekko fitted shirt with the rebel flower on it. Yael opted for slightly more respectable flair; she's wearing a men's black tuxedo jacket she pulled from one of the closets, sleeves rolled up, paired with a long forest-green rib dress, and a velvet knotted turban headband in the same green that's helping keep her curls in a low bun. She's like a Marlene Dietrich throwback, and our grandmother would have been delighted.

'I've been thinking about it and I don't think you should stay here, in Hobart,' I say.

Yael frowns at me, and it's like watching a light begin to dim as I see her assume the worst.

So I'm quick to explain. 'You shouldn't come home, because then I'll be all alone in Sydney – and that would really suck.'

And just like that, the wattage turns up. It begins in Yael's eyes, and then her lips are curving and her cheeks bulging, but she's still not saying anything so I ramble on.

'I mean – if you wanted to, we could maybe find somewhere together. An apartment, I mean. I figure it's time I put those film royalties to good use, and while I decide if I want to study, or work or, I don't know, maybe audition somewhere . . .'

And then Yael is unbuckling her seatbelt and flinging her entire body across to me, so I have to catch her with an '*oomph!*' as she bear-hugs me and I have no choice but to wrap my arms around her right back.

While we pause like that, her chin resting on my right shoulder, and mine tucked into her collarbone she talks so I can't see her face.

'I'd really, *really* like that,' she says.

And I don't mention that she sounds a little waterlogged. I don't even say anything when she pulls back and swipes quickly at her eyes, at the happy tears collected there.

'What brought this decision on?' she manages to ask once she's sufficiently fixed her eyeliner with the tip of her finger.

I shrug and say, 'Courage, Dorothy,' remembering Riya's affection for *The Wizard of Oz*. 'I figure it's time I stop being scared to want things again. Even if they're maybe the same dreams I had when I was young, and getting them the first time round didn't exactly go to plan . . .'

Yael nods, and then rolls her eyes towards the block of houses belonging to Riya and her family. 'Well you're on a roll, so you better keep going.'

And with that, I unbuckle my seatbelt, get out of the car, and cross the road to Riya's front door, and knock three times for luck.

THIRTY-SEVEN

The door swings open to a familiar face in the process of throwing his arms out and excitedly saying, 'Happy Diwali!' But then his arms fall to his sides and his smile falters when he sees me.

'Arin, hi!' I say to Riya's cousin, who I haven't seen since the party where she and I first met.

He's wearing what must be traditional dress – a long, high collared tunic top in bright ochre colours, with loose fitting pants underneath.

'Ellie! Hi!' he says, once he's over the shock of seeing me. 'Is Riya expecting you?' I shake my head, about to say more.

And then behind me more people in tunics and sarees in beautiful jewel colours come bustling up the stairs in a clamour of silk and aromatic trays of food. I bump into the little balustrade by the stairs as I move to let them through, and the whole while they're shouting, 'Happy Diwali!' as they brush past Arin and then he says, 'Wait right there!' He closes the door and dashes inside.

I don't know what else to do but look behind me to Yael parked across the street. She has the window wound down and her head is poking out, staring wide-eyed at me, and then she gives me two thumbs up and I smile.

'It's you.'

I swing back around to find Riya standing next to Arin, who pops a piece of cake into his mouth as he looks between us intently.

'It's me,' is all I can think to say.

She's wearing a saree in deep azure with gold trim, and her hair is down in a riot of curls. Her eyes are delicately kohl-rimmed and she's wearing red lipstick. She looks stunning.

And then – nothing. She stares at me, and Arin stares at me and nobody says a thing. The sun is starting to go down and casting us all in a buttery haze of pink awkwardness.

'Um, Happy Diwali?' I try, pathetically. 'I went to the Cinema and they told me you'd be here, celebrating.'

This seems to shake Riya out of her silence. She looks to her cousin, who gets the hint and turns away as she steps out onto her little porch and closes the door behind her.

As I come back up from the step to stand level with her, I smile nervously. 'What is Diwali anyway? I've heard of it, but I'm not sure I know . . .' I trail off.

'Festival of lights – or the triumph of light over darkness, good versus evil,' she replies, in a clipped tone.

That stops me short because, *wow* – how fitting.

Riya hugs her arms against the sudden drop in temperature, and then she huffs in annoyance. 'Ellie, I am sorry for your loss, but I can't do this right now.'

I shake myself a little and start talking. 'I know it wasn't you who told the paper. We actually found out it was one of the disgruntled ex-husbands. In hindsight, we probably should have rounded up the usual suspects and figured that out.' Riya's face doesn't register the *Casablanca* reference at all, but I carry on. 'I think I knew it wasn't you. In fact, I know I did – but I still lashed out. Because I'm maybe a little broken, with good reason to be. But someone very wise recently told me that I have to remember that not everyone I love will hurt me.'

At that, I think I see a slight change in Riya's face. I continue, buoyed by a little increase in courage and the realisation that this could be my last chance.

'And I think you should know that you scare me. A lot. Which is ironic, considering I'm the monster in this equation – in more ways than one. But you do, you terrify me.' I can feel the tears coming, but I blink them back and keep talking. 'I think I'm suddenly getting why you love horror movies so much. The adrenaline of that – of being close to the thing that scares you the most, it's . . . amazing and intoxicating and I want to jump out of my skin most days. I want to scream. I really want to run, but I think there's something in sticking around. Walking down the stairs when you hear a bump in the night. Skateboarding down the street, looking for trouble. Confronting the monster in the end. Standing in front of the girl you hurt.'

I stop for a second. I'm breathing heavily and my hands are clammy. It's also – like a typical evening in Hobart – just started drizzling in a fine mist. I swipe a hand through my hair self-consciously and position myself a little more in front of Riya, to block her beautiful Diwali outfit from getting wet and to keep her under the tiny little awning of her front door. But the change in weather won't stop me. I need to finish this.

No matter what happens in the end – I need her to know.

'I get it. I do. Being around the thing that scares you the most, it can sometimes make you braver and better, and . . . because I know that I'm a better and braver person when I'm with you.'

Riya opens her mouth, then closes it. She's frowning at me and deep down, I know that can't be a good sign. I take a step back, stick my hands in the pockets of my slacks and shrug my shoulders, about to cut my losses and take my wounded heart home.

But then she's dropped her hands from hugging her arms.

She's stepping towards me.

Reaching for me.

I take one step forward and she meets me – her hand wrapping around the back of my head and pulling me towards her mouth for a kiss that's mostly teeth as we miss slightly in our excitement. But then we find a rhythm pretty quickly. My whole face is slippery from the rain, but she licks some of those droplets that collect on my lips and it makes me laugh.

What breaks us apart is Yael honking the car horn excitedly and repeatedly, sticking her head out the window of the wagon to *woo-hoo!* from where she's parked across the street. And then like something out of a ridiculous romance movie, strings of fairy-lights I hadn't even noticed before now are switched on, lighting the front windows of Riya's house and the outline of her doorway.

We giggle and Riya looks over my shoulder to give an awkward finger-wave Yael's way. Then she turns her lips back to me and

I'm opening for her, little by little until she pulls back again to whisper.

'You scare me too.'

'I'm sorry.'

Riya shakes her head. 'I'm not.'

THIRTY-EIGHT

The skies are inky black and filled with stars. It's cold but the forecast is clear.

And the State Cinema is completely packed for Halloween.

Or – so I'm told. I can't really tell from the rooftop, and because they haven't started letting people in yet. But I can just spy them over the edge – spilling out onto Elizabeth Street. Cars have been halted momentarily, and Riya is down there somewhere helping out with crowd control. I think I can hear the doors open, and the streaming chatter of hundreds of people being let in down below.

I take a deep breath and spin around to find Mum, Jasper, Yael and Poe already in their front-row deckchairs and facing the big rooftop screen. They're rugged up, but keen.

Fright Night for Final Girls are here too but they're a little more relaxed in beanbags off to the side. Currently Kate is doing a pretty good job of aiming Maltesers at Ah-Pei for her to catch with her mouth, arms going straight up in the air with each goal, and then a mini-competition seems to be starting between her and Maria.

They're all armed with registration forms for membership sign-up, and they'll be working the crowd once they get here.

Jen catches my eye and signs something to me, and I raise my hands to reply, holding my arms horizontally in front of my chest and making my index fingers crawl. Probably the perfect sign for indigestion, butterflies and a general feeling of creeping dread. But Jen just signs back with both hands fisted in front of her face, *you got this,* and I hope she's right.

And then the glass elevator dings and Riya steps out, striding towards me and smiling. She's in uniform, but also with her purple raincoat on against the cold and pinned to her collar-tips are two wolf-heads, smiling with big teeth. She says a brief hello to my family, then approaches me.

She kisses me quickly and pulls away, but I grab the sides of her raincoat and bring her back for one or two more before she laughs and we break apart.

'You ready?'

'No.'

She reaches up and cups my face in her hand gently. '"Beware; for I am fearless, and therefore powerful" – remember?'

I nod my head, but what comes out of my mouth is less sure. 'I think I'm going to throw up.'

Riya drops her hand to take both of mine in hers and brings them up to rest between our chests. 'You're among friends and family, and people who understand that horror is the one genre that puts women's fears and insecurities under the spotlight, only to be overcome.' She clutches my hands. 'And we are all here for you.'

I love the way she talks. I love her passion. I love her. And if AFTRS don't accept her into their music composition program this time around, I'm going to have serious words with someone and get her butt to Sydney anyway, so she can start preparing for the next round of entries.

I take a deep breath and Riya squeezes my hands. 'Better?'

'Always.'

'We've started letting people in via the stairs and elevator, okay? Once the rooftop fills up, everyone else will go to the regular and basement cinemas. We've got your microphone feeding into all those rooms, and then the movie will begin.'

'I got this.'

Riya makes the same sign Jen did, and says, 'You got this!'

She dashes away again to control the crowds and collect tickets. Given we sold more than enough to book up the whole State Cinema for this one event, we've cleared the amount we needed to invest in a better titling program.

But I know not everyone is here just for me.

They've come for Lottie, mostly.

To pay their respects and remember her. I read somewhere on the internet that fans even wanted to bring their cricket bats along and hold them aloft in tribute, even though it's not *The Hazards* they'll be watching. The cinema politely requested people leave their bats at home, and instead they invited everyone to come in costume as a tribute to their favourite of Lottie Lovinger's film and television oeuvre. So there are plenty of zombies milling about, people dressed in slinky evening gowns, or short-shorts. It's a little bit surreal seeing so many imitations of Lottie among the crowd as they begin pouring in. But it's also beautiful, and

I can't wait for the end of the evening when the owner of the cinema will announce that they'll be naming this rooftop space in her honour.

Suck on that, Errol.

'You ready, cousin?'

Yael pokes her head around the big white projector screen, and when I turn to smile at her she comes to stand fully before me. She spent a not inconsiderable amount of time arranging her hair in kiss curls – taking locks and curling them onto her hairline then plastering them down with gel and hairspray, so they frame her face in soft tendrils. She kept referencing old black and white photos of Josephine Baker to get it just right and they look incredible.

'I think so,' I reply to Yael's question.

The hair-do is really nothing compared to Yael's outfit this evening: an inky black, floor-length, bias cut, smooth satin gown with tight, geometric panelling around the hips. If it were warmer, she'd have shown off the exposed back too, but as it is, she's thrown on a burgundy-red velvet tuxedo jacket that takes absolutely nothing away from her own Lottie tribute. Because it's one of the most iconic dresses Lottie ever wore in her career, and it helps that we have an in with the costume designer from the film, *Seven Hills*. And if any Hollywood puritans are gasping in horror, they can rest assured that Poe had to make a dozen variations of the gown – this is just one that Lottie took home, and Poe was able to alter to Yael's specifications. Now it looks like it was made just for her, and she seems to glide in it.

And then she does just that, coming to stand closer to me as she frowns and asks, 'Then what's that face for?'

Damn, and I thought I was hiding it well. I close my eyes and take a deep breath, imagining a balloon expanding in my chest with every exhale – but then Yael gently touches my shoulder and I look at her, see the questions behind her eyes.

'What are people going to think? In the months, or years from now when I talk about what really happened and how Lottie let me down? Are they going to believe me, if I get up there this evening and say all these glowing things . . . ?'

Yael sighs in sympathy. 'What is it those little film geeks have been saying all this time?' She says it affectionately, and with a small smile. 'Something about how horror is the one genre where women are allowed to be as they actually are? Imperfect, messy, sometimes good, sometimes bad, tough, selfish . . .'

'Monstrous?' I add, to which Yael nods and continues.

'Well, maybe in the future you tell people to apply a little of that understanding to the real world too. That we contain multitudes. And for that reason, it is nobody's goddam business if they choose not to believe you, because they can't wrap their heads around someone being both loving and conniving, beautiful and terrible. Complicated, beloved – and missed.'

And then Yael wipes delicately beneath her eyes, at the tears that are making tracks, and regardless of her immaculate outfit I reach out and pull her into a fierce hug, and she wraps her arms around my back.

And then the rooftop is all but filled up – and the FNFG sign of Riya and Jen doing *The Scream* comes up on the screen, a beacon in the night illuminating me and Yael so we break apart, smiling at each other with watery eyes. I watch her walk back to our family and the rows of deck chairs, which are now filled with a hundred or so eager faces looking to the screen I'm currently hiding behind. Riya comes to get me, holding a microphone in each hand. We kiss and it's quick, but sweet. Then we rest our foreheads together for a beat before she goes to greet the crowd.

'Good evening, everybody, and welcome to this special event screening of *Blood & Jacaranda* hosted by your local Hobart Horror film club, Fright Night for Final Girls . . .'

There's a wonderful silence before the crowd erupts into thunderous clapping. Some people also wave their hands in the air, the Auslan version of applause. Riya and Jen have to wait for their noise to die down, all hands to lower, before they can begin again.

I tune the rest out, concentrate on my breathing and beating heart and turning my eyes to the skies that are stretched out endlessly up above me, and then I hear my name. Riya appears, ushering me forward to come and stand with her in front of the crowd. It's dead quiet again, only the distant sound of North Hobart traffic down below, white noise in the background. And I'd almost forgotten how exhilarating it is to be in front of a crowd.

'Ellie Marsden, everybody!'

It's not just the rooftop that cheers, but we can hear the sound from down below too – what must be them foot-stomping, hollering and clapping long and loud so we can hear them.

I vaguely hear Riya's words once the cheers die down. She is explaining that there will be a Q&A portion after the screening, but first Ellie would like to say a few words.

And then it's over to me.

I bring the microphone up and it screeches momentarily, and I apologise, but when I bring it back and start talking it's fine. Everyone reclines in their deck chairs with anticipation, and I can feel the lights of the building beaming up at me as I begin.

'Hi everybody, and every Lottie' – that gets a few laughs, and I make a show of squinting into the crowd before continuing. 'I want to thank you all for coming out tonight to support this wonderful and inclusive film club, a cinema that's a national treasure, and above all else – for my grandmother, my *bubbe*.'

I grip the microphone in my hand, find Yael's face in the crowd – Poe's and Mum's too – and I just tell the truth. 'I loved my grandmother – very much. I still do. She was not perfect. She was complicated. Not "I-have-to-lop-off-my-undead-husband's-head-with-a-cricket-bat" complicated like she was in the movies' – that gets another laugh – 'but the regular kind. Ambitious to the point of selfishness. Ruthless and single-minded. Vain and secretive. She sometimes felt suffocated by her family legacy, which I can relate to. And she experienced her share of tragedies in her time. But she also saw something in me that no one else did. She encouraged it and encouraged me to play – to be in my imagination as much as possible. She told me I was brilliant, and I believed her. And for a very little while, I got to play make-believe with her, in this movie we did.'

A few people clap spontaneously and loudly, and it jars me for a second. From the corner of my eye I think I see Riya make a move – I don't know what she thinks she can do, so I give her a small shake of my head and she stops. I clear my throat and go on. 'I know it was scary for a lot of you. It was scary for me too, for such a long time. But I'm not scared anymore.'

I need to wrap this up, because I'm losing it. I can feel the tears coming and my heart beating and I need to confront this monster already. Let it in, so I can finally get a good look at it.

I exhale and say, 'So without further ado I give you *Blood & Jacaranda*.'

And then I'm going to Riya, who takes both our microphones and switches them off. She lays them down on a table and wraps an arm around my middle. Then she walks us to the back of the rooftop and two more-private seats where she takes my hand, and never lets go as I sit with my fear for a little while.

I do this for me, and no one else. To prove to myself that it won't control or define me. Fear is not my finality.

And I will be the one left standing in the end.

A NOTE ON THE (FICTIONAL) AUSTRALIAN FILM HISTORY

The world's first feature film was Australian.

It's true.

The Tait Brothers from Victoria made the very first feature-length film – *The Story of the Kelly Gang* (1906). It first screened in Melbourne's Athenaeum Hall, which was owned by their family. The brothers were among many pioneering Australian filmmakers throughout the silent era – including Lottie Lyell, Raymond Longford and the McDonagh Sisters.

But the 1920s saw a new era in cinema in the dawn of 'talkies', and commercialisation of sound movies. And this period also marked the death of Australian cinema.

Suddenly there was a barrage of Hollywood movies flooding the market. They had higher production values, bigger stars, the ability to meet fan-demand at an amazing turnover of production and were more easily distributed to our cinemas because the Americans had control over all major distribution companies. Hollywood had more money and better technology, coupled with their inherent glitz and glamour, so it was nearly impossible for local Aussie filmmakers to compete, or even get a foot in the door of their own industry.

In 1928 a Royal Commission was even held into Australia's movie decline, but it merely pinpointed the problem and came up with few solutions. And by 1951, the government had introduced a new rule against raising capital for companies, which further wounded the already struggling industry.

Between 1952 and 1966, Australia was averaging the release of two films a year, and those were mostly co-productions with other countries (with some notable exceptions, like the 1953 film *Jedda* starring Ngarla Kunoth). This also explains why the few major Australian film stars from that time – the likes of Errol Flynn, Diane Cilento, Peter Finch, and Oscar-winning costume designer Orry-Kelly – all had to go overseas to make their mark in the movies. There was the odd, exceptional story of Australia playing host to Hollywood. In 1959 director Stanley Kramer adapted Nevil Shute's novel *On The Beach* and stayed true to its Melbourne location. Gregory Peck, Ava Gardner and Fred Astaire filmed all around Port Phillip Bay, and Gardner apparently cursed up a storm at Frankston station in between takes – much to the amusement of crowds and extras.

What saved the industry from vanishing completely was intervention by the Gorton and Whitlam governments in the early 1970s. Prime Minister John Gorton created the Experimental Film Fund and the Australian Film Development Corporation, both of which fostered an independent Australian film industry, and increased government funding for the arts generally. Gough Whitlam's government further built on these foundations by creating the Australian Film Television School (AFTS) and establishing a Film and Television Board as one of the initial specialist panels in the new Australia Council for the Arts. Later it became the Australian Film Television and Radio School (AFTRS).

Both of these changes to the culture, funding and investment in our film and television led to a 'New Wave' of education and creation. Australia produced nearly 400 feature films between 1970 and 1985 – more than we had ever made before. Many of these films are today recognised as classics worldwide, but they also went a long way to shaping modern Australian identity, both at home and abroad. *Picnic at Hanging Rock* (1975), *Mad Max* (1979), *My Brilliant Career* (1979), *Breaker Morant* (1980), and *Gallipoli* (1981) – to name but a few. They put Australia and our creators on the map, and marked our stories as 'worthy' and worthwhile. They gave us a voice we'd never had before. And they let us see ourselves, finally.

But it's still sad to think of the films that weren't made, and the talent that was lost for those long years that Australia did not have a cinematic identity. This is why when I began writing this book, I decided to envision an alternate filmic history for ourselves. One in which we were making movies right alongside Hollywood.

I took a fair bit of inspiration from the Barrymore acting dynasty, in imagining the Lovinger family as being at the forefront of this Aussie filmic enterprise. I chose to make-believe an era in our film history, when revolutionary costume designer Orry-Kelly could have dressed a Lovinger descendant for a local production, in between working on *Casablanca* and *The Maltese Falcon*.

So much was lost and derailed before our government realised the power of investing in the Arts, and what can be gained when a nation is allowed and encouraged to tell their own stories, and examine their own past, futures and identities. I simply chose to play within a fictionalised timeline, when the cultural and educational investment in our artistic industry was always there – making movies and magic with Australian stories on the silver screen, during a Golden Age that never quite came . . .

ACKNOWLEDGEMENTS

I wrote a chunk of this story in isolation and then lockdown, while the COVID-19 pandemic raged around the world and then here in Melbourne. Suddenly a book about death, grief and trauma became 100 per cent harder to write – funny, that. But what I kept coming back to – what kept me going – were the words of Brooklyn-based writer Talia Lavin, who Tweeted on 26 March 2020, *If you're writing or editing or working on a book right now, it may be incredibly difficult because the future is so uncertain. But every word you put on paper is an affirmation of the fact that there will be a future. It's a profound act of faith.*

She was right.

To that end, I'd like to thank the communities formed around stories in their many forms, and an abiding belief that they matter. Those who ensured I never felt alone. Thank you to all those in the Australian Arts – the creators – and especially to those of book publishing; the bookshops and booksellers, directors, controllers, editors, designers, publicists, readers, agents, reviewers, teachers, librarians . . . and all those who reminded me what would be on the other side. Thank you.

A special shout-out to the Oz Authors Online (OAO) crew. We had an idea and made it into a celebration of our book community. Thank you Wai Chim, Anna Whateley, A B Endacott, Shivaun Plozza, Jenna Guillaume, and Jin Wang – legends, all.

To my authenticity readers – I cannot thank you enough, and I'd like to acknowledge that any slip-ups and mistakes therein are now all on me! Retu Kaskana – thank you for the clarifications and suggestions, but especially for the swear words (and thank your cousin for me too!). Fiona Murphy – it meant so much to me to get the Auslan right and true; thank you for helping me with that. Rachel Gillis – for all the information and guidance on Jewish representation and customs. I hope I did okay in the end. (And thank you to Meg Moores for connecting us. You're both such champions of YA, thank you for that too!). Sarah Robinson-Hatch (of 'The YA Room'!) – I've been such a fan of yours for so long. It meant the world to me that I got to share Ellie and Riya's story with you and listen to your thoughts and feedback.

Thanks also to Manda Diaz – for your very good DMs and knowledge about the National Film and Sound Archive of Australia. Appreciation for Carly Findlay too – there's nobody I'd rather lean on or have lean on me.

And Jacinta di Mase – for continuing to be the badass I aspire to one day become.

Kate Stevens for believing in this one despite my early ineloquence. Bella Lloyd for being the best publicist an author could ask for (even during a pandemic!). Jeanmarie Morosin for your guidance and wisdom on seeing this through. Claire de Medici and Samantha Sainsbury, for so much help with the story and edits. And Karen Ward, who has become integral to the whole process for me. I could not do this without you.

Thank you to Anne Barnetson for my beautiful front cover. I wish this was the 'Take On Me' music video and Ellie and Riya could come to life and walk off into the moonlight together.

Mum and Dad (and Murray) – every book is for you, and because of you too. Mum for your sharp editorial eye in particular. And Dad, for coming on a research trip to Hobart with me that helped immensely. We had a wonderful time in particular watching *Knives Out* at the fabulous State Cinema. If you're ever in town, you simply must visit! I also thoroughly enjoyed popping into The Hobart Book Shop, Fullers Bookshop, State Bookstore, Dymocks Hobart and Rapid Eye Books.

To Laura, Lisa, and Claire especially – Yael is my small tribute to all of you, cousins I am so thankful to also call my friends.

To the entire Balaam, Binks, Brooke, Fowler, Jenkins, and Porter families – we experienced so much loss and heartache throughout 2020 and said goodbye to many pillars of our family. Omi, Pat and Don especially – I miss them, but I could not be prouder or more thankful that they were ours. I intend to do them proud.

I thought a lot about grief, loss and trauma while writing this book, and I hope I articulated the struggle in some small way. A certain monarch once said: 'Grief is the price we pay for love.' It's true.

I love all of you.

Danielle Binks is a writer, reviewer, agent and book blogger who lives on the Mornington Peninsula. In 2017, she edited and contributed to *Begin, End, Begin*, an anthology of new Australian young adult writing inspired by the #LoveOzYA movement, which won the ABIA Book of the Year for Older Children (Ages 13+) and was shortlisted in the 2018 Gold Inky Awards. *The Year the Maps Changed*, Danielle's debut middle-grade novel, was a CBCA Notable Book for Younger Readers 2021, longlisted for the ABIA Book of the Year Award for Younger Children 2021, shortlisted for the Readings Children's Book Prize 2021 and longlisted for the Indie Book Awards 2021. *The Monster of Her Age* is Danielle's debut YA novel.

www.daniellebinks.com